GOING

By the same author

The Man Who Got Away
Edens Lost
Careful, He Might Hear You

Sumner Locke Elliott

GOING

HARPER & ROW, PUBLISHERS
New York   Evanston   San Francisco   London

FIRST EDITION

Designed by Patricia Dunbar

Library of Congress Cataloging in Publication Data

Elliott, Sumner Locke.
  Going
  I. Title.
PZ4.E4645Go3 [PR9619.3.E44]   823   74–1882
  ISBN 0–06–011242–5

GOING

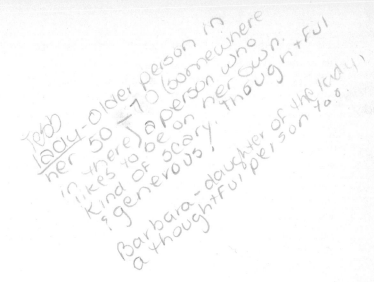

Today was the day.

And I must be ready for it, she said to herself, getting up when the alarm went off. Not because she wanted every precious minute of it but rather that she wished to be a step ahead of everyone today. So she would have the prerogative; so she would be down before anyone else, so she would be waiting. There would be something privileged about being ready and waiting, dressed and ready with everything done, everything tidied, put away. As if she didn't care what was going to happen to her.

And she would say to Barbara, "There's some toothpaste and cold cream left over," as coolly as that and thereby she would draw a line between her and their vulgarity. She would not accept their vulgarity and their loving-kindness today; it was her prerogative. So she bathed and dressed, put on a soft blue dress from the remains of her finery and a big straw hat that had once been heaped with taffeta cabbage roses and much admired, and put on her last good pair of gloves.

Then she took out one by one the rest of her dresses and suits on their hangers and laid them on the bed to be given away to whatever deserving cause her daughter might find. And this too would be a

I

reminder to them that she had been thoughtful and organized right up to the last minute.

So she laid out her clothes and straightened things on the dressing table and took a last look around the room where for the years since her husband's death she had been kindly allowed to live.

Then she took her old Mark Cross crocodile bag and made sure that she had everything she would need right up until seven o'clock that night: handkerchief, lipstick, cigarette lighter and ballpoint pen (though what would she need to write down?) and especially her glasses, she could not read a thing now without her glasses (though what would she need to read *today?*), and the little leather case with the photograph of her husband. It would be nice to take it out and look at Elton if she wanted.

Then she opened the door and went downstairs with her hand on the rail because there was a little shakiness in the back of her legs, but that was the only sign of any actual physical fear.

Nobody was up and she had her house to herself. She glanced into her drawing room, which had been gathered together with such care and in her day had always had great crystal bowls and silver vases of flowers, and where in winter they always had splendid fires. Nowadays on Fridays from nine to twelve ugly stumpy stands were brought in, looped to each other with imitation velvet ropes, and groups of tourists clumped through (part of the arrangement that her son-in-law, Harry Platt, had made with the Department of Housing whereby the house had been saved from destruction and they had been allowed to continue living in it; no, not *them* so much as Harry: Harry Platt was allowed to live there) and stared around while a guide told them the house had been built in the 1930s, over sixty years ago, by a Mr. John Adams, who owned it outright, and that it was later occupied by his daughter and son-in-law, a Mr. and Mrs. Elton Bracken, pointed out the high ceiling, the carved fireplace, which was actually used; the curious object in front of it was an ornamental fire screen. The floor-to-ceiling bookshelves had once held books. At this point the guide usually remarked the fact that with all the reading these people did, they had had pollution, crime

2

in the streets, venereal disease, political corruption and anarchy.

Once, forgetting it was Friday, she had come into the room in the middle of a tour and they had stared curiously at her in her old-fashioned tailored clothes as though she were one of the relics that went with the tour, this elderly woman wearing her hair pinned in a little ball on the top of her head and not basin cut, and all touched up with makeup, and so, relic that she indeed was, she had stared back at them all as though she might for a moment be mistress, hostess once again and then she had said, "Excuse me," and turned and walked out and heard the guide say, "That was Mrs. Bracken, who is still living." A little titter had run through the group.

Now she crossed her drawing room, still a little shaky in the legs, and went through the terrace door into the garden and was instantly affronted by the brightness of the morning. The day was as clear as glycerin; so clear and clean that it hurt the eyes to look at the sky. They had cleaned the atmosphere so efficiently that mornings often had a merciless quality so one could see every leaf, every brick on the path, each stem. Yet the clean air had no taste; it had the no-smell of air conditioning. Occasional shrubs were plastic.

And down the nestling hills the plexiglass condominiums ran, cheek by jowl all the way to Mount Kisco. Where the little cathedral of pines had once so delighted the eye from the end of the terrace, there was now the ugliness of GLORIUS PX 105 with its circulating towers. But if she kept her eyes focused directly ahead, her garden remained intact, if foreshortened. The tennis courts were gone but there was the barn, here was the old gazebo (she rested a moment on her old garden seat nobody had bothered to paint for years); here were the tubs of azalea and petunia and the pots of fuchsia and impatiens she doggedly planted each year to keep a sense of continuity, a link with her own time as frail as the leaves themselves.

Water still dripped into the abalone shell.

Dearest (her husband had said on the tape rather hoarsely), do forgive me but I don't terribly want to go on with this any longer. . . . She had done what he requested and immediately destroyed the tape so that there would be no absolute proof of suicide to endanger her, because there were severe punishments handed out nowadays to survivors. But the voice remained in her mind. It often cruelly unwound itself in the silence of her loneliness.

Now as she looked down into the abalone shell where the bright green moss moved, Elton's hoarse voice said, "Do you remember the day you slipped and fell on Vesuvius? And the fireworks over the Bay of Naples? Perhaps we should have been busier looking out, who knows? I'm glad it happened; thank you for slipping. I'm terribly sorry about this, cowardly of me, dearest, but I'm just too tired, Tess, I can't go on with it, darling."

Surprisingly, because there were so few of them now, a butterfly flew past her and she made a motion in the air to grab it and hold it in her hand to feel the beating of its wings a moment; she would have liked to feel that little pulsation of life and then to let it escape.

Escape, escape, she wanted to say to it, fly away. Because didn't butterflies have an extraordinarily short life? It was one of those things, if she were going to be around, that might be worth looking up. But she wouldn't be around as long as the butterfly. Now, she thought, if I had a prayer it would go something like this: Let something happen at the last moment to prevent it because even *now* it is all too precious to lose.

She got up and walked a little way across the lawn and bent over to pick a clover (because just supposing it was four-leaved: that might be a sign) and then knelt on the grass and said aloud, "Listen, God or whoever, let something happen at the last moment, could you? Even if I had to be sent away somewhere to some bitter-cold island it would be better or it might *seem* better. But if you can't, then for God's sake don't let me be shaky at the last. Let me have the courage to get through the damn thing with dignity." There was a loud bang instantly. A shot? She almost fell on her side, then scrambled up.

Only the kitchen door banging and her daughter Barbara coming toward her with that aggravating walk Barbara assumed nowadays, an unctuous crablike walk: she swung from side to side, she swung as she walked like a canoe slipping through rapids. She was wreathed in dreadful smiles.

"Ah, there you are," Barbara said.

She was extremely agreeable all the time now; she was almost too much to bear.

She slipped an arm affectionately through Tess's and her stiff disposable paper dress was as harsh as emery on the skin. "Did I startle you?" Barbara asked and did a ridiculous thing, took hold of Tess's chin and waggled it. "Were you—were you having a little prayer?"

"Good *God*, no," Tess said. "Who, *me?*" and moved ahead imperiously and said, pointing to her tubs and pots, "Now these must be watered every day. I don't want you to forget."

And felt sorry for the poor thing lumbering beside her, poor Barbara with her pepper-and-salt hair basin cut and the hideous paper dress on which the dreadful cheap hibiscus pattern had been imperfectly stamped and so looked as though it were gouts of blood, as if Barbara had been soundly whipped. As though Barbara hadn't been whipped enough.

"Ah," Barbara said. Sometimes she said, "Ah, *fancy.*" She was so converted. She had a nervous tic of a smile; if you caught her lost in thought or frowning she flashed this terrible smile. "Ah," Barbara said. She was driven by willingness to accede and Tess knew that Barbara was also willing that there would be no scenes today because scenes sent her into fits of nail biting and sometimes to shaking all over and moving her lips soundlessly in one of the new prayers; this woman who had once lived and thrived on passionate arguments and voiced vociferous opinions and defied and castigated, marched.

* * *

"Peace," Barbara said.

"Oh, peace is a word," her father said.

5

"So is war."

Barbara, hair flying around, eyes on fire, biting into a plum and spitting out the pit.

"Darling, don't do that. Spit things out on the table."

"In my opinion," Barbara said with her mouth full, "Hitler wasn't any worse than Truman dropping the atomic bomb on innocent civilians."

"Darling, we had had Pearl *Har*bor."

"There's no excuse for any war, ever."

"Do you know how many American boys were killed at Pearl Harbor?"

"Well . . ."

"Darling, don't shrug at me, please. Because you can't shrug off Pearl Harbor or Hitler and you are only trying to make me angry and you will not make me angry, Barbara, you will not!"

"You were not *in* any war."

"No, but—"

"So you know nothing about war."

"I know what we had a responsibility to *do.*"

"You just theorize, sit in the Harvard Club with those fascist fat conservative pig friends of yours—"

"We had a responsibility and furthermore—"

"Go sit safely in the Harvard Club with your fascist friends while we're throwing people out of airplanes because they won't betray their own people."

"Furthermore, I find it a bit illogical that you kids go around preaching peace and all you do is blow up places and endanger people and condone violence. That absolutely appalls me, really sickens and appalls me—"

"I'd very much like to blow up the Harvard Club."

* * *

6

Well, they'd let her sink in the quicksands, poor Barbara, hadn't they? Well, no, not quite. They had put up some kind of fight, hadn't they? The details were hazy in her mind, it seemed so many years ago, but she remembered Elton protesting violently to Harry and then later there had been some struggling when those buxom nurses had come to take Barbara and she, Tess, had hit one of the nurses in the face.

She bent and picked three sprigs of lavender, partly to disentangle herself from Barbara's arm. "Smell," she said and waved the lavender under her daughter's nose. Barbara had slipped into a limbo moment and was frowning, puzzled, as though she had been trying to connect with some lost perimeter of herself. Caught, she lunged away as though the lavender were a knife and then flashed on the smile.

"Ah," Barbara said. "Mmmmm."

In the kitchen this strong girl sat, wearing the blue uniform of the Ladiesaid, a mug held up to her mouth.

"Ah," Barbara said, "here's Hooper." Then Barbara said unctuously, as if she hoped she might get approval from Hooper, "It's all right. She was in the garden."

Ladiesaid! They'd promised and gone back on their promise that she was to be spared that.

"How do you do, Miss Hooper," Tess said and held out her gloved hand. They didn't like you to call them Miss or Mrs.

"Just Hooper, honey," Hooper said.

She was as undistinguished as a sheep in her regulation blue with the fake silver buttons and her badge with the photo of herself on it and she had little pink rabbit's eyes behind her steel-rimmed glasses, but her handclasp was the same as getting your hand caught in a bear trap. She possibly had a zip gun in her bag and her smile went right into you without warming you in the least. Squads of these young women, Tess felt sure, were led onto a field every morning to do smile exercises.

"Well, honey," Hooper said in a whiny voice, "I feel I know you already, I do indeed. I feel right off now we are going to be pals."

These volunteer women, an army of drab souls, mostly spinsters or unqualified to do specialized work, were detailed to older people now like unwanted nannies to give comfort and aid to them in their final days, driving them around, reading to them, playing cards with them. But everyone knew they were there to keep an eye on those who might be tempted to do something rash with themselves and upset the notion that they were pleased to "go" and give space to others, propagandized as the supreme act of selflessness and accompanied by a letter of acclamation from the President. Ignored was the fact that these buzzards were a constant reminder to the elderly that their days were numbered.

"Now I'll just have to look in your bag, honey," Hooper said, holding out a beefy hand for it.

She had the rudeness to open the leather folder and look at Elton's picture.

Shook Tess's lipstick to be sure no capsule was concealed in it.

Handed her back her bag.

"That's all right, then, honey."

"Breakfast," Barbara said.

On the table was a pear.

Nobody referred to it.

She saw Barbara's quick averted look as she poured coffee; the pear was her expensive gesture, a salute, farewell. It must have cost her dearly, more than the astronomical cost of pears, the cost to herself, and Tess was warmed by it and would have liked to have said something, kissed her poor psycholobotomized daughter, but she knew she mustn't.

"Hot muffins, doodles," Barbara said.

Barbara twitched her stick arms here and there over the table, arranging the tasteless muffins, the coagulations of what passed now for condiments and jellies, and she and Hooper talked across Tess with that peculiar predigested conversation that always sounded like a tape recording talking to another tape recording, never ventured an opinion, vaguely suggested, agreed, made abundant use of the words "goodness" and "gratitude." How nice the new Condimart was at the new Bedford multilevel, how perfect the weather was. Tess wondered about the strain on them, why more of them didn't go shrilly berserk with this constant suppression of irritation and anger. They were everlastingly grateful, glad; they sang praises; everyone was such a wonderful human being, so kind. Of course, they *did* go berserk once in a while and started screaming in the Condimart and throwing things and shouting obscenities, cursed the President and God too and ripped off their clothes in the walking zone, but they were quickly subdued and tranquilized or in the worst cases shuttled off to places like Sea Island, Georgia, where Harry had had Barbara sent away kicking and screaming and from where she had returned smiling endlessly, boneless, filleted.

"I sure do love these little pastry doodles," Barbara said. "Wouldn't you think they were pastry?"

The Hooper girl said she would indeed. Mercy, it was simply wonderful what they could do these days to make you think you were eating anything in the world.

And now in the door came old Zeekie, lurching, blind in one eye, quite deaf, and even oblivious to squirrels these days. In came old Zeekie and rocked drunkenly toward them, slavering.

"Oh, the old dear," the Hooper girl said.

"This is old Zeekie," Barbara said and cooed to him, "Did you want your din-din, Zeek?"

He gave her a worn paw. He regarded them haughtily through his one eye, his tail thumped once to appease them, but he was beyond fussing over them now. His dignity was immense in spite of his deterioration and smell.

"Oh, he's just a big sweetheart, isn't he?" Hooper exclaimed, her pinched face softening; she was almost human about dogs.

"Well, I should say he is," Barbara cooed. "I should just say he *is*. He is a real person, that's why."

"How old is he?"

"Why, he's almost seventeen."

9

"Seventeen! Oh, my. *That* old."

"Poor old Zeekie, he's getting very feeble. It's probably cruel of us to keep him but—"

"Oh, I know, I know," the Hooper girl crowed. "You can't bear to have him put to sleep."

"Can't bear to," Barbara said and then flushed crimson right down to the back of her neck. But there was nothing anyone could do (she knelt, desperately stroking the dog to hide her crimson face) to help her over the gaffe; it was merely part of the absurdity of the situation, the juxtaposition of dogs and humans, humans put to sleep, dogs living to seventeen.

But it was nice that Barbara had seen the irony in it. And she had bought the pear.

Tess cut into the pear. It was hard and woody.

At the same moment they heard the chopper directly over the house and saw the trees bend and flatten, shiver as if in apprehension of Harry Platt's coming and then five minutes later they saw the bubble cart bobbing into the driveway and the chauffeur hopping out to open the hatch. It was a mistake, Tess thought, to have allotted Harry such a tall chauffeur; it served to emphasize Harry's shortness. Harry stepped out. Now there ought to be a drum roll, she felt, sensing the importance of him even at a distance; even at a distance the emanation of importance was such that it evinced drum rolls. Harry Platt marched toward the house with his peculiar gait. It was said to be impossible but there it was: he actually swung his right arm with his right leg, left arm with his left leg—left/left, right/right. It called for sympathy if one had dared. But on the other hand it called for guardedness, this animated-doll walk, neat little feet in highly polished lace-up shoes, pompous walk of this short man in the prim navy suit that could have come from Paul Stuart way back in the Nixon days; spic and span, priggish tie with the White House clip. Harry Platt burst on them as he had always done, like someone jumping through a paper hoop. His quick small feet came up the front steps and then sounded clipclop across the marble of the hall and instantly an intercom phone rang in his study (it was chilling

10

how efficient was their timing) and the house reverberated with importance. Barbara ran. The Hooper girl was terribly impressed; she gave a tug to her uniform jacket. "Oh, my," Hooper said. "He's smaller than he looks on television." Well, he had arrived and all her invocations had been for nothing (could she have got hold of some incense, she would have burned it), her fervent hope that Harry would be kept in Washington; the benison that on this her last day she would not have to see Harry Platt.

Workmen had come and sawed and hammered and cut holes in the roof of what had been Elton's study and the result now was theatric, to say the least, because Harry was raised up, desk and chair and all, on a graduating series of small levels and illuminated by a glass skylight that in these days of merciless brilliance bathed him in a radiance that was exactly (although one would not have dared mention it to Harry) the color of urine. He was so self-satisfied, he was so actually pleased with the skylight and the effect it had on people coming into the study, that he was quite boyish about it, he turned this way and that in his swivel chair, which was made of the finest almost unprocurable glove leather, and his boyish smile was of such delight that only the snidest or the rashest person in the world could have said to him that he was bathed in light the color of urine.

P's and *q*'s were minded. People praised.

Except for his wife, who in one of her exceptional moments of sobriety said, "Why, Harry, we are seeing you in quite a different light," Joan said and Harry's look of displeasure was made even more liverish in the golden light.

"Well, Tessa," Harry said (it was one of his little conceits to use this sobriquet; he reminded her every time he did so she was merely a chattel). "Tessa, how *are* you?" Harry said and it would take someone of Harry's bottomless insensitivity or else deliberate spitefulness to ask such a question of her today. How are you? The question for people on the steps of the scaffold was not how were they?

Another indignity was this shaking of hands. You had to shake hands with Harry, Washington speech writer, adviser to the President, son-in-law; no matter, you *had* to shake his hand. So Tess did so, leaving on her white glove. She had to stretch up her arm a little, so high was Harry on his throne in the yellow light.

"Well, now," Harry said, glasses on, no time to waste no matter what else was going on in the house, in the world, no matter who was being "called for," shuffling little important clean hands through papers. "Well, now, Tessa, what can we do for you today? What is on the agenda for today?"

He didn't mean it, of course, to be offensive. He smiled at her; he was completely charming. He had very good teeth and a little cleft chin and a slightly retroussé nose that could mislead you into thinking that somehow they added up to trustworthiness.

"Now is there anything special you would like to *do* today?" Harry asked obligingly. "Is there any little treat I can arrange for you? Would you care to zip down to Florida this afternoon? Is there anyone you'd like to see?"

She would have liked to see her grandson but that could not be mentioned.

"I would like to see Lacey Edwards," she said.

"Absolutely," Harry said. "Is there transport?"

"Oh, yes, oh, yes," Barbara said. "They sent a lovely girl."

Tess dared to say she would be pleased to go by cab. It was only to Mount Kisco.

"Oh, we couldn't let you go by *cab*," Harry said. "We have to think of your comfort," Harry said and flipped an intercom and spoke to somebody sharply in Washington, to some underling cowering at the other end about forgetting to stamp a number on a stet card. A minute insect, a midge perhaps, basked in the sun on the sea of warm mahogany and as Harry barked irritation into the phone over laziness, incompetence, he brought a finger down and ended the midge's life and this minuscule murder appeared to soothe him because he flipped off the intercom, smiled his warmest smile (the one most to be cautious about) and told them a little human interest story about the President, about Mrs. Dudley Ward (Harry had been present in the Oval Room) receiving a group of children representing some association (Tess was minding her *p*'s and *q*'s and she scarcely listened; one of life's tiny revenges was to only pretend to listen to Harry) and of how this charming thing had happened. This little girl was so awed by being with the President, she dropped the bouquet and it was an awkward moment what with the television cameras there and then the President herself had saved the day by stooping and picking up the bouquet and kissing the little girl. Just the kind of thing, Harry said, that they couldn't have prepared for her to do, the kind of dear warm human gesture she was so capable of. Ah, Barbara said, ah.

She had picked up the bouquet herself.

And now I would like to tell *you* a story, Tess thought, smoothing her gloves, about a little *boy*.

The little boy with the flower bud of a face who was being put on the bus to be taken away to PERMCARE. He was screaming and crying, protesting with all the puny strength he could muster in his little arms and legs. "No, no," he screamed at the cajolings of his parents and the neighbors.

"No, no, I won't go," the little boy screamed.

"Now, Sidney," the young father said.

"*Sid*ney," the mother said. They wore smiles of patient tolerance.

"Your own playmates," the father said.

"A lovely dormitory," said the mother.

"No, no," the child shrieked as the bus driver tried to take hold of him and the people standing around chortled.

"No, no," the little boy shrieked.

"Oh, he's cute," a woman said.

"Some of them get such fancies," said another.

Tess had pushed her way through the knot of people and clutched the sobbing little thing to her. "Don't cry, darling," she had said, hugging him and kissing the little wet face. "Don't be scared, now, sweetheart, nobody's going to hurt you, it's only school, baby, and it's not so bad, don't cry, don't cry." The way the child clung to her so desperately with beseeching eyes, she thought madly for a moment of running away with it, but where? And they were already closing in on her. It had been quite a melee, separating her and the child, as the men pulled her by the arms and the women took hold of the kicking, screaming child, who was handed to the bus driver. The bus roared off. They all looked at Tess reprovingly. "What's the matter with you, lady?" the child's father said. "You shouldn't do a thing like that; it's cruel." "You have to make them *go*," the mother said. "You can't be soft with them."

Tess lifted her hands weakly to ward them off.

"Oh, you people," she said. "I'll never understand you. I don't *want* to ever understand you." She ran.

"Old," someone said.

"Just can't cotton, can they?" someone said.

Harry was saying now that it was the little things like that that counted, the child dropping the bouquet.

She thought of all the little things that had happened to them since Harry came into their lives and that she, like so many others, had just let them happen and now they were coming for *her* in a bus and there were only just these hours left and anyway nothing could make a scrap of difference now, not even if this moment she picked up the sharp paper knife and stabbed Harry to death because there were Harry Platts all over now. Every fifth person was a kind of Harry Platt.

Joan leaned in the doorway.

"Oh, hel*lo*," Joan said. She was in her nightdress, holding a cigarette; her face was puffy from last night's drinking. She had no makeup on, her eyes were only little dots, her mouth a button; she had the dazed look of a just-awakened baby.

"Oh, look who's here," Joan said. "If it isn't the master himself." She twisted around the door, hair matted and falling over her eyes. "If it isn't the lord and master. What a thrill, what an honor."

"You have no robe on," Harry said, vinegary in the urine light.

"I *thought* I heard the official helicopter," Joan said, "or did you come by molecular transport? What's it like being sent by telegram? I believe they're having trouble getting the kinks out of that, did you know? It's like being sent by telegram, Mother. I hear some poor bastard had himself transmitted to Seattle and they left out a digit and he was reintegrated without his torso."

Harry had come down from his desk and was standing to attention in front of his wife, feet in first position, arms at his sides, his smile barely enduring her, rather as though she were talking through the national anthem and he would just wait for the anthem to be done before he hit her.

"You would be careful, Harry, wouldn't you?" Joan said. "I mean, if they have you sent anywhere by molecular transport, I mean, to make absolutely certain, honey, that they send *all* of you. I mean, *picture* my grief if some part of you was misplaced. Oh, picture my despair, honey, if they lost some of you."

"Now, Joan," Harry said quietly. His eyes glittered now. "Now, Joan, we would rather not have nonsense today, O.K.?"

"Who is talking nonsense? I am deadly serious."

"Now, Joan, why don't you get dressed for a change?"

Joan had been kept a deep dark secret for years. Only the immediate family knew about Joan and she had not, as would ordinarily be the case, been sent away to be dried out and put through behavior modification because of the risk that someone might discover she was *the* Mrs. Harry Platt.

So when Harry's home life had been filmed for television, an actress of whom nobody had ever heard in their lives was engaged to portray Joan, wearing dull clothes, and sat with her arm linked through Harry's, reading off a board the flat remarks that were expected of her and being precisely the kind of wife the country would expect of Harry.

Meantime Joan, who had been kept under lock and key upstairs, opened a window as the television crew and staff were leaving and screamed, "Help! I am Anastasia, last of the Romanovs, kept alive on vitamins. I know where the jewels are."

"Why don't you get dressed, Joan," Harry said quietly. He had taken hold of her elbow; he was pulling her arm around.

"Why don't you spit on me?" Joan said loudly. "Why don't you take that goddamn sanctimonious smile off your face? Oh, do it, hon. Why don't you take off your goddamn smiling Sunday face, Harry, and let's see the real one, that looks like a warthog."

"Now, Joan."

"Oh, come on. Be a pal and show us the real Harry, with all the warts and the little bristles poking through your ugly little snout."

Now he had her turned to him in a parody of an embrace; face to face, they seemed exactly like an old-fashioned Spanish dance team about to begin a flamenco, except that Harry had Joan's arm twisted and fitted back into her spine so that if he wanted he could snap her arm in two.

"Get the key, Barbara," Harry said quietly and Barbara ran on flat feet.

Joan, pinioned, turned her head this way and that casually, like a slightly curious turkey the moment before the ax comes down. She blinked at Tess and then said, "Why are you all dressed up?"

Then, in the moment Harry started walking her, pinioned, sideways, all bent over, crabwise out of the room, walking her detention-camp fashion, Joan had begun to scream backward to Tess, "Oh, my God, Mother. Are you being put to sleep? Is it today? Oh, my God, is it today?"

Harry was getting her upstairs now, pushing her ahead of him and speaking to her all the while in the implacable, unperturbed voice they all knew brooked no insurrection; all the way, as he forced her stumbling ahead of him and now giving little cries of pain, all the way Harry smiled like a church usher.

Tess came to the bottom of the stairs.

"Leper," she called to Harry.

* * *

Long afterward, somebody said this young man had apparently just walked in on the tennis party from the outside; just strolled in from the road out of the pine grove. What was definitely established was that long after dark somebody heard Jim Myers calling out from the changing room in the pavilion behind the courts, "Somebody get my pants. I'm stuck here with no pants." So it had been learned this boy who had wandered in had come up to Jim and said, "Can I borrow your shorts for one game?" and the crazy thing was Jim took off his shorts and handed them over but the boy never brought them back. Joan Bracken later told her mother she *felt* someone staring at the back of her neck, felt the little prickles of it, and turned around and saw this young guy leaning on the stone drinking fountain and he gave her a very strange smile just as if he knew everything about her; it made her uncomfortable because she found she could not *help* turning around from time to time and there he still was, had not moved from his position, and each time he flashed her this knowing smile. Then without anyone remembering how, he had inveigled himself into the last doubles of the day when Barbara Bracken's partner got stung by a wasp. Suddenly out of nowhere there was this odd-looking boy in a pair of tennis shorts too long for him, swinging somebody's racket, offering to pinch-hit; nobody wanted him but as he stood there looking eagerly from one to another, nobody had the nerve to say get lost, who are you anyhow? O.K. if I play? he asked and the next minute he was partnering Barbara and somebody later told Tess Bracken it was fascinating, it was like watching somebody who had heard the game of tennis minutely described but had never actually seen it played: the way he ran (he was flatfooted and his thick gray woolen socks emphasized it) this way and that so eagerly as if the world depended on it and the way he wriggled his buttocks waiting for the serve, scraping at the gravel with his flat feet. "Exactly like a little sowlet in heat," Joan said. The way he almost knocked himself out, running to lob, to return; ran flatfooted; the way he marched across the court was comical: his right arm moved with his right leg, left with his left. It reminded someone of Jacques Tati; there was a good bit of suppressed laughter and the boy seemed to sense it. Once he made them all a stiff little bow.

Joan was suffused with laughter. "Oh, he's so ridiculous; oh, I

17

think it's probably the gray socks more than anything that's the perfect touch." Joan was currently bewitching Andrew la Farge of the oatmeal cereal la Farges and she hung onto Andrew and rocked back and forth, brushing her long fair hair against his face.

Then the set was over and Barbara and Jacques Tati the losers but the boy was not content to walk off; he had to shake hands with all three, bowing from the waist with a stiff humorless bow and quick clamp of the hand.

Then everyone walked back up toward the house and left him standing by the courts alone.

So naturally Tess was astonished, glancing out of the library window, to see him standing alone in the garden, hands in his pockets and looking like a lost bird in his cheap brown windbreaker. There was something pathetic about him hanging around still; even the impertinence of it was a little touching.

Tess opened the door to the garden. Instantly he wheeled around as if caught red-handed doing something, looked frightened and then obsequious. He bobbed his head at her, grinned.

"Hello," he said.

"Hello," she said. "Were you waiting for someone?"

"No," he said.

Now it would have been opportune to say they were about to serve supper, about to sit down, and so politely hint but firmly get rid of this gate-crasher. Yet for some reason she couldn't; pinned by his eyes fastened on her, waiting, she couldn't nerve herself to do it.

(And afterward wish to God she had snubbed him well and truly then and there, shown him the gate.)

"Well," she said, "we're only having easy sort of franks and beans but won't you have something with us before you go?"

He bobbed his head at her. "Oh, that would be all right," he said. He was condescending; he might almost have said but couldn't she run him up an omelet?

He stumped along beside her.

"I don't believe we were introduced," she said. "I'm Tess Bracken."

"Harry Platt," he said. He stuck a hand out at her, which she was obliged to shake.

"Harry Platt," she said to the group of young people drinking on the lawn (and she saw that *he* saw there was a little pot being smuggled around and that he disapproved). There was some sniggering and Joan had fallen onto Andrew la Farge's chest with what seemed a kind of seizure. But hardly an eyebrow was raised. They were a well-bred bunch.

Then Joan was heard to say clearly, "Some people need a brick wall to fall on them. Somebody go get a brick wall."

"Harry Platt," Tess said to her husband, "is going to have a little food with us."

Harry Platt shot out an arm, practically clicked heels. Elton looked surprised. But no, not a drink, Harry Platt said. He didn't drink.

Someone was sent to fetch bitter lemon.

"Who brought him?" Elton asked.

"Apparently he drifted in."

"Nervy."

Harry Platt stayed for supper. He was consistently ignored. He sat down at one of the groups of tables and was crowded out and glanced at only when he passed salt and pepper or ketchup to someone but he joined in heartily whenever there was a burst of laughter even though there seemed to be no amusement in his eyes and after dark when Elton turned on the light on the statue of Aphrodite which this year Tess had grown a bed of dark blue pansies around, Harry Platt looked puzzled as to why anyone would go to the bother of lighting up a statue and putting pansies around it. It seemed quite beyond his comprehension; in fact, he seemed a trifle disconcerted about it.

He was conspicuously helpful at the end, running back to fetch forgotten raincoats and tennis rackets; he rushed ahead and held open doors of cars for the girls to get in and remembered everyone's name. Good night, Ellen, he said. Good night, Lois. "Mrs. Bracken," Harry said very formally, "may I express my thanks for an enjoyable evening."

"Sir," Harry Platt said to Elton, "may I express my thanks for an enjoyable evening."

Then he marched down the drive with his peculiar walk; even more peculiar was Tess's stifled impulse to say they had been delighted he could come.

Then Hannah, cook and lifelong friend, said, why, goodness, his father owns that secondhand car lot off Route 9, the one with all those ugly signs and little flags the conservationists have been trying to get rid of as an eyesore and young Harry has an old utility and does odd-jobbing. He'll do anything, Hannah said.

"I can believe it," Tess said.

Well, for one thing he has an ice machine and delivers ice cubes, many as you want; so he had delivered ice cubes that afternoon round about four, Hannah said.

Well, they laughed over it for the rest of the week and told the story on themselves, taking care not to make it sound snobby. Joan was especially funny telling how the iceman cameth.

Harry Platt faded quickly from their minds; they might almost have had to be reminded who he was when the doorbell sounded on a Sunday afternoon that was ginger colored and lashed by driving rain.

"Did you know your sprinklers are on?" he asked. He looked drenched, looked as though he had swum Lake Michigan to tell them this, his yellow slicker ran pools in the doorway, and before Elton could say anything one way or the other he had darted off into the perpendicular rain and they could see from windows all around the house the yellow slicker running from place to place to turn off the sprinklers. Then he appeared back at the front door, panting for breath.

"Well, thanks," Elton said. But no more.

Harry Platt, running with water from every hair on his bare head to squelching shoes, had had either the humorlessness or nerve to say, "Mr. Bracken, could I have a glass of water, I wonder." And sat in the vestibule dripping and sipping and talking to Elton with great respect and a good deal of calling him "sir" until Tess came to the rescue by saying Elton if you don't get dressed this minute we're going to be late.

"Good-bye, good-bye, good-bye. Going, going," Harry Platt said heartily, backing into the downpour, and then plunged back. "Oh, nearly ran off with your glass, ha, ha," putting the glass on the floor for her to pick up.

"I wonder how he turned the sprinklers on without us seeing him?" Elton asked.

Nothing so mundane as running into Harry Platt in the supermarket or in the newspaper shop made the dinner-table conversation— after all, he presumably needed bread and freeze-dried coffee and toilet tissue as everyone does—so it was not deemed important enough for any of them to remark that Harry Platt was standing in the next line at the post office; was also buying *The New York Times* when Barbara was picking up theirs; happened to be emerging from the pharmacist's at the time Joan was going in and elaborately held the door open for her but she cut him dead. But it was, Tess began to think, the accumulation of these little meetings that began to oppress her very mildly, just like the beginnings of a headache so slight one isn't even sure whether to bother with an aspirin; a kind of tiredness, a depression at the sight of the short, alert figure waving, saluting, bobbing, appearing out of nowhere full of little good deeds, to point out the only vacancy in the parking lot (just happened to park a minute earlier and saw them coming and held the place); outside the movie house to inquire solicitously had they enjoyed the movie? From time to time she began thinking she saw Harry Platt where he was not, so felt deflated for a second and then blown up with relief seeing it wasn't Harry after all.

Whereas Joan was perpetually diverted by the very sight of him, perpetually sent into spasms of laughter and driven to mockery, as if he had prepared himself to be her sacrificial lamb in public. Everything Harry did, said, wore sent Joan away on a roller coaster of hilarity. Oh, she would gasp, he's got on suspenders *and* a belt; I didn't think they still did *that* in Kokomo, *Indiana*. Oh, my God, Joan would scream, stop the car. There's Harry Platt with a *girl*. Oh, I've got to see this to believe it. Back up, will you, so I can see what the poor thing's got wrong with her. Oh, she has to at least have acne ten inches deep and a cleft palate to have to be going out with Harry Platt!

Sometimes it seemed as if Joan had taken up this game of hunting down Harry Platt with intent, the way she could spot him from great distances (as she had done the first time at the tennis court, *sensed* him), from the back of her neck. Standing, gossiping idly, bored with the girls perhaps outside the drugstore in Mount Kisco, Joan's eyes would suddenly widen, her pupils narrow to slits, catwise, and she would say I don't want you to turn your head around yet but I am a living witness to a sight you will not believe because Harry Platt has on a leather coat and leather boots like he is one of the real boys and he is coming this way. Keep looking at me as if we don't see him because he is dumb enough to think we might be noticing *him* but just as he comes past take a look and you will think you have freaked out!

And when they roared past Harry plodding along the lanes and byways, Joan would lean out of the station wagon and call, "Hey, there, iceman," and he would shoot her a quick wary look and then wave and if she looked back he was still waving; it was comic and pathetic, the sight of his stocky little figure waving as they raced away.

"Uggghh," Joan would say, wriggling. "What a little worm. Uggghh, imagine if he *touched* you."

"Would you care to give a guess who our barman is tonight?" Elton asked on the evening of Barbara's birthday dance in October. Of course, Tess knew even before she pushed open the flap of the big pink-and-white-striped tent; white jacket, little snap-on black tie, hair all slicked down and even slicker story about how Joe Canna (their barman for sixteen years at every large party they ever gave) had been rushed out an hour ago to White Plains outpatients with an impacted wisdom tooth. Harry Platt blew out his cheek like a balloon and swayed about to show the throes of agony Joe Canna was in. He had brought with him four large canisters of free ice cubes; he was very happy, he said, to fortunately have been free to step in in this emergency. He'd brought along an assistant, a pimpled and seemingly permanently abashed creature to whom Harry gave orders snappingly, snapping fingers and all-of-a-sudden-terribly-efficient and quite dictatorial ("Kenny, *Ken*ny, ice, twist-of-lemon, Tabasco, soda, hurry it up") when the guests started arriving: bourbon and soda, snapped Harry, Scotch-rocks, vodka-quinine, on the double, Kenny. For names he remembered, Harry obligingly mixed drinks himself.

"Oh, *no,*" Joan said and aped swooning on Andy la Farge. "Oh, no; promise me on your dying word of honor that I am seeing things. Oh, the *worm,* burrowing his way in," Joan said. "Just watch me put him down. *Bar*man." Joan was cruel. She ordered an esoteric drink she'd had in Barbados. It required the meticulous blending of white rum and three ingredients. Harry was unfazed. Ah, but alas, they had no grenadine. But listen, he would mix her a Passion Flower, which was practically the same only with bitters. The moment, as was noticed by her squires, had not been Joan's. This might have been the reason that much later on Joan could have been seen at the bar exchanging conversation with the barman, who lit her cigarettes, and whenever anyone tried to drag her away to dance she said no, no, I'm talking to Harry. Joan prefaced everything she said with "Tell me, Harry . . ." and appeared to be deeply interested, even impressed, by what Harry had to say and those not familiar with Joan's deviousness could not have surmised that she was planning anything. She let Harry light her cigarettes and fill her glass and waited to see what garden path she could lead him up. Harry's scrubbed face was pink with pleasure, a dew of triumph glittered on his forehead at the homage being paid him, such attention being paid him by this Nereid (let his fingertips just touch hers accidentally),

23

until Joan coaxed him to tell his little joke to the whole group (he only had one joke, Harry told her solemnly, but it might amuse her, he said, stop him if she'd heard it, he pleaded honestly with her, anxious beyond anything to please, and if Joan had been kind she would have stopped him then and there; anyone would have had the heart to stop him because it was the oldest joke in the book and even Joan's generation had heard it in their cradles; it would have been a humane act to stop anyone from telling it again) and Harry began the story so pleased as punch and so deadly sincere that it practically caused a riot but more of groans than laughs and the effect it had on the whole bar was as if they had all been given emetics and were trying to throw up; oh, man, that is a yock, they assured Harry, that is *always* a sure laugh, they said and Harry saw the derisiveness in Joan's smile and took a cloth and very carefully wiped down the bar until they had moved away and there was a small dignity in the way Harry wiped down the bar so assiduously; it might almost have suggested that in point of fact the laugh was on them.

Evidently Barbara Bracken thought so. "What a lousy thing to do," she said to Joan.

Barbara tramped over to the bar. "Hello," she said to Harry, who was still wiping down the bar. "Would you dance with me?" Barbara asked.

As he turned her round and round flatfootedly on the dance floor, Barbara certainly held Harry too deliberately; she had already begun to take up causes and she danced with Harry as though he were a cause. She held him with one hand knotted into a little fist behind his neck as though she would punch anyone who came near him. They were the unlikeliest couple ever to be on a dance floor, Barbara holding onto Harry as though he were a cause and Harry holding Barbara like a broom and staring past her into some void that seemed to be filled with fires of hurt, and so they circled joylessly around the floor, Barbara's sharp chin up in defense of barmen who told stale jokes and the barman with eyes riveting into some future all lit up with fires of hurt that would one day set alight this house, perhaps the world. So they tramped around the dance floor,

24

him treading on her dress, her fist knotted into his neck.

"Oh, why must she do that?" Elton asked. The vein in his forehead was pulsing as it always did if there was something ruffling the placid lake of his status quo.

Joan was laughing too loud, gratingly.

"Joan, come here a minute," Tess said.

"I'm not talking about Joan," Elton said. "I'm talking about Barbara. Dancing with the *barman.* I'm democratic, God knows, but—but it's not the kind of thing I find . . . graceful. God knows I'm not a prig but why feel you have to *do* such a thing and there are young men here tonight in evening dress and *pink shirts."*

His vein pulsed at the creeping vulgarity of it all.

So it was that Harry Platt became Barbara's friend. Nobody quite knew what the relationship was. Certainly there was nothing carnal about it but even without that it seemed incongruous, it was hedged around with certain ambiguities: Barbara was a rebel, seizing on every rebellious cause she could find, waving them like swords; Harry was conservative and gentle. Harry went to church on Sundays. Harry expressed devotion to God and country. Harry stood up instantly when the anthem was played and placed his hand across his heart. Barbara got up grudgingly and continued to eat an orange. Yet they entered into this curious relationship and Harry came to visit Barbara on Sundays. Every Sunday. They stayed apart from Joan's friends and from Tess and Elton's friends but they were a nuisance in the way plasterers might have been a nuisance, having to be stepped over sitting on the staircase or on the front steps. They were also insufferably exclusive, which made people feel left out. Come into her own drawing room with guests, there Barbara and Harry would be, stretched out on the sofa, and they would get up and stalk into the garden, annoyed at being intruded on; come into her dining room to serve iced tea, there would be Barbara serving Harry her ugly untidy bologna sandwiches on Tess's best china, Harry lolling in Elton's chair at the head of the table. Sometimes Tess had to rise from bed and call into the dimly lit hall that it was way after midnight, only to be given no reply.

"I notice he never takes you out," Tess said.

"This is my house, isn't it?" Barbara asked. She had grown increasingly rambunctious. "Or am I under some misapprehension?"

Joan reveled in it. "Barbara's friend the ice cube vendor," she said to everyone, pointing him out. "Do you suppose they're *doing* it?" she asked Tess. "Ugleugleugle," Joan said, making sounds of vomit. "Ugleugle. Imagine being in bed with *that*. Oh, my skin creeps. Oh, my pores close."

Joan passed by Harry without a look or word, in the manner of Eleanor of Aquitaine passing by a serf in a narrow doorway. But Harry was watching Joan.

Seeming to be intent on Barbara, his Siamese-cat eyes would wander to wherever Joan was. When Joan came into the room his body would stiffen; he would stretch and flex his muscles and then he would laugh his humorless clackety-clack laugh, which approximated a train crossing an iron bridge. Watching Joan, he stroked his strong, hairless arms while Barbara, totally absorbed in converting him to whatever her latest crusade was, didn't appear to notice that he slipped away every so often and came back, mentally slipped off her leash for a minute or so and wandered like a wolf in the night.

One twilight, Tess came around a wall of privet to see that Joan had left a yellow sweater lying on the croquet lawn; saw just in the nick of time that Harry was coming from the opposite direction and (more and more now, this humiliating hiding from Harry; one was constantly slipping hastily behind hedges or into a guest bathroom to avoid him) she stepped back and watched while Harry stopped to pick up the sweater; watched fascinated while he glanced around and then held the sweater out by the arms as though Joan were in it, as if he were holding Joan and about to dance with her. Then knotting the sweater into a ball, he thrust it into his groin; then turning so now Tess could see only his back and the squirming motions of his buttocks but even at this distance she could hear the gasps and moans he was making of misery or delight; he weaved a step here and there, back and forth as he moaned and looked up at the sky, all the time performing this convulsive dance; then he turned around and held the sweater at arms' length and Tess thought she had never seen such a look before on anyone's face, emphasized by this bottle-green light of fading day as Harry began twisting the arm of the sweater exactly as though it were Joan's own arm, all the time running his tongue over his lip and smiling, twisting until the arm bone would have snapped long before.

Twisting, twisting, and whistling through his teeth.

"I don't want Harry to stay for supper tonight, Barbara."

"Why not?"

"I just don't want him tonight."

"Why not?"

"Take him out to a diner or somewhere."

"Why?"

"I don't want it, Barbara, and I don't need to give explanations every time I don't want something."

"Why don't you want Harry?"

"I just don't."

"Isn't this *my* house too?"

Alone in the house on the Labor Day weekend, Elton away fishing, Joan with the la Farges on Cape Cod, Barbara pressed unwillingly into going to Amagansett with a long-neglected friend, Hannah off, she heard the front doorbell ring and thought heavily, there he is. Closed her eyes, lying on her bed in the cool air-conditioned bedroom where she had been reading, appropriately, *A Room of One's Own,* waited while he rang, then rang again. Now, windows all closed, all shades drawn down, surely, surely the house must seem deserted and surely after a while, she thought, even Harry will go away. So when after ten minutes the ringing stopped, she got off the bed and went to the window and, drawing the curtain an inch, she peered down at the front portico. He was gone. Then just as she got back on the bed, the kitchen doorbell buzzed angrily and kept on buzzing, on and off for about five minutes, and oh, God, she said, thinking suddenly of Thomas à Becket, who will rid me of this troublesome priest? She bade her body and mind to lie still, relax, ignore by the trick of thinking only of running water, and tried through the buzzing, over and over buzzing, to keep her mind on the page she was reading until he would eventually go away, must have known by now that no one was home. The buzzer at last faded into silence. She gave a sigh of relief at the same moment as he began insistently ringing the side doorbell. He was making the rounds of the house. It would stop, then begin again; there was nothing to equal his persistence. But then, this was Harry Platt.

She leaped from the bed and, red hot with anger and a kind of exuberance, she ran downstairs. By God, she said, let me get rid of him now once and for all while I am good and mad.

She flung open the door so wildly she almost fell on him.

"There's nobody home," she shrieked. "Nobody's at home, Harry. Who do you want?"

"Barbara."

"Barbara's away."

"I thought she might be back; she said she might come back a day early. . . ."

"She's not here. We're not in. What do you *want?*"

He took a step backward, gazing at her mildly.

"What do you *want? Who* do you want?"

"I just thought Barbara—"

"Why do you pretend to come visiting Barbara?" she shrieked. She took a step toward him; he retreated a few steps backward down the drive; he seemed smaller than ever in the heat of her rage. "Why do you pretend it's Barbara when it's Joan you want to be with? Anyone can see, a blind dog can see it's Joan you come here for. What do you *want?*"

"Nothing."

"What do you want? Why do you come here all the time? Why do you bother us all the time? Why can't you see Joan wouldn't look *sideways* at you? Why do you persist? Look, I have to be blunt: we don't want you coming here any more. Mr. Bracken and I don't want you here any more. Now go away."

But the way he looked at her, abashed, like a poor stray dog being shooed away from the door in a blizzard, eyes full of hurt and genuine bewilderment, she had the craziest moment of feeling he was a victim and of wanting to run and caress him, comfort the poor kid because the way he looked, he probably never had a loving word said to him in his life; probably had a drunken mother who beat him. This was the dangerous emotion Harry Platt brought out in women; it was almost akin to mother lust.

That was the dangerous thing about Harry.

"Go away, Harry," she said.

And slammed the door on him.

* * *

"Now, then, here we go."

Hooper, the Ladiesaid volunteer girl, took her firmly by the arm as though she were being arrested but Tess shook her off and said, "Don't do that; I don't like being touched. I'm not going to run off." Hooper relaxed her grip but kept hold of Tess's elbow as they walked toward Hooper's car. "Where do you suppose I could run to?" This was certainly true. Her age was stamped on her identity card, on her ration card; she couldn't last a week. At sixty-five you were "called for" and put to sleep. It was said the anesthesia tasted of peppermint and caused momentary exultation. People were said to die laughing and singing.

The sky blazed in the clean noontime air. A jumbo Trigger passed silently overhead like a laser beam and the programmed cars went by on the radar belt, silently and all at the same speed.

Hooper programmed her car and off they went.

As they passed the hideous GLORIUS PX 105 Tess said, in order to discomfort the Hooper girl, "See there? I can remember when that was a hill on our property and on summer nights my mother gave concerts there, string quartets. My mother was a cellist and you've no idea how beautiful it was on moonlight nights in a little grove of birch trees hung with white paper lanterns. Little white moths would flutter around the lanterns and we sat on pillows on the grass while they played Mozart and Vivaldi and Reger in the moonlight."

"Oh, well," Hooper gurgled indulgently, "if you like that sort of thing."

"It was all so graceful, so lovely," Tess said, "you can't imagine."

"Just think, now you can have all that on capsule," Hooper said. "You can have two hundred hours of music on one little capsule."

"But not with white birches and moonlight," Tess said, "not with little night moths like ghosts."

"Oh, I suppose," Hooper said.

They were all insulated against beauty, against humor, against music, against *thought*. Oh, God, Tess thought, I'm glad Elton's dead, I'm glad Daddy's dead and all the people like them. I'm glad Zina Edwards is dead.

She looked at Hooper, who had plugged into the radar belt and had sat back now doing some crocheting of a particularly ugly spinach color; looked at Hooper's young unlined face, a dutiful face unmarked by woe or desire or passion; expressionless as uncooked pastry. She wanted to say to Hooper, Haven't you ever cried your eyes out? Haven't you had a mouth on your mouth with tongues mingling in delight? Haven't you had a man's legs around you?

"What do *you* like?" she asked.

"Band music," Hooper said. "I've got over a thousand hours of brass band music."

In Mount Kisco Proper, which was now a minicity, Hooper disconnected from the belt and switched to self-drive and they passed along streets of ugly high-rise units until they came to where a large old house had been left standing. A sign read BIDING. FOR MATURE AND SENIOR PERSONS.

Surrounded by high walls, deceptively charming, this gracious old red brick house rambled over acres and was set about with additions and with chimneys, verandas and cool porches appearing unexpectedly, grape arbors gone to seed; moss on the front steps, geraniums, so innocuous-looking you expected children's bicycles piled near the door, expected friendly dogs to come leaping out.

Expected friendly faces, greetings, embraces.

"Aha," said the youngish matron, fixing Tess with a beady eye. "Have you a visiting-privilege card, dear?"

"She's allowed to see Miss Edwards," the Hooper girl said and gave Tess a little nudge forward. As always, the reaction to the place had been so awful she had had to lean against the door for a minute: the sight of the taupe walls, intended to dull the senses and discourage the soul, the revulsion to the terrible ugliness of it all and to the unspeakable vacancy of the faces that looked up apathetically as she passed through the room; surely they must be partially sedated, these people sitting around a television set or listening to cassette books with earphones. Had you screamed Fire, nobody would have moved. But then they might have welcomed fire. This was one of the waiting places where those approaching sixty-five or those who were retired but with no family and therefore stamped "unwanted" were assembled to await their euthanasia.

And, Tess thought, if it hadn't been for Harry Platt and his importance, this is where I would have been.

"Come this way, dear," the matron said, bustling ahead to lead Tess into a weary little visitors' room. The President of the United States, Mrs. Ward, smiled from the wall.

A sign read: OBSERVE KINDNESS.

When the nurse brought Lacey in, it was obvious they'd given her special privileges for the occasion. She had on one of her own dresses. It was too short and little-girlish, showing her bony knees, and she had put on a lot of eye makeup without her glasses and lopsided, giving her a Picasso-like look. She had tied a ribbon in her white hair.

She and Tess kissed.

"Now we'll leave you together," the nurse said, "and trust you girls to be on your best behavior."

"Look at the ass on her," Lacey said as the nurse squelched out in her rubber shoes. "They all have asses like water buffalo."

They sat down on a creaking wicker settee and Lacey said, "Do you have any cigarettes?" Tess took out her last pack and Lacey gave a squeal. "Oh, *real* ones. I haven't tasted anything but dried seaweed filters for months."

Lacey sucked eagerly on the cigarette. She was wearing a lot of rings and bracelets that had belonged to her mother and that Tess remembered, especially a large aquamarine. She dangled amber earrings. It would have been more tactful if Lacey had not decked herself out and had simply acted as if this were Tess's usual monthly visit.

"Did you bring me anything?" Lacey asked.

After all, Lacey was only a little less than sixteen months younger than Tess and her euthanasia draft number would be coming up within a year. When it absolutely had to be referred to, they called it jury duty. So-and-so got jury duty, they said.

"All I've got left of my old paperbacks," Tess said.

"Oh, thanks, oh, marvelous. You should hear the dreadful junk they've got on cassette here." Lacey grabbed the decaying old books, some of which were turning to yellow dust.

Hooper had come into the room and dragged a wooden chair to a distance where she could observe but not quite overhear. She took out her ugly crochet work.

"Who's that?" Lacey asked.

"That's my guard, Miss Hooper," Tess said in an undertone.

"What huge *breasts*," Lacey said loudly because breasts was not a word used in the new prim society; even on television commercials, breasts of chicken had been euphemized to "chests."

And now, because they'd been allowed this last visit together, it seemed they had little to say to each other; they were like two people at an airport, one seeing the other off and the plane delayed. They smiled weakly and asked each other dull questions and gave dull answers. Lacey even stifled a yawn and tears oozed out of her made-up eyes. But then Tess saw more tears dropping and that Lacey's mouth was sucked in to hold the sobs and she turned Lacey toward

32

her so Hooper would not notice. "Hold on," Tess said under her breath. "It's all right, dear. I'm quite calm. I'm managing quite well."

"Oh, God, Tess," Lacey whispered. "I just realized I won't have *you* when *my* time comes and I'm going to be so *frightened.*"

* * *

Funny how they had become friends. It was all accidental and at one point in their young lives they had swapped mothers.

Tess had taken the wrong raincoat. She was in such a hurry to leave the dance (it had been one of those affairs where they were referred to as "the young people," so it was easy to figure out the kind of arch conviviality that would be forced on them) that when they said her father was waiting for her she flew out of the ballroom and into the bedroom where perhaps a hundred coats lay in a mountain on a bed like dead bodies piled up after a holocaust, and unearthing what she thought was her raincoat had fled down the stairs, not even saying good night to anyone, and it was such a relief to see Daddy waiting in the hall that she had called out all the way I'm coming, I'm coming and then hurled herself at him, embracing him. Is there a fire, is there plague? Daddy asked.

She hadn't wanted to go in the first place. Imagine going to anything called a Sweet Sixteen Party in the year 1946. She said she wouldn't know anyone there except the girl it was being given for and whom she knew enough not to accept seriously. Said this girl was a square and that she and her family spoke with such a well-bred lockjaw accent you couldn't understand a word they said (she did an imitation of the mother: "How or yew, moi dear? Terruffic!") and implied, moreover, that the brother was said to have got nine Radcliffe girls pregnant. Well, Tess, Daddy said, the chances of your being raped on a blazingly lit ballroom floor in the former Wyankopf mansion seem to me to be remote. "Anyway, they are, not *special,*"

33

Tess said. "Why waste one's time with people who are completely not special?"

She disliked the dress Mother got for her. It was her first real party dress, pale lettuce green organza with a big sash and terribly, she said, June Allyson and she thought of swallowing a little salt water and being able to throw up dramatically just as she was leaving and then Daddy came in and made her close her eyes and fastened a little necklace of real seed pearls around her throat and kissed her and so what could she do but go?

And in the taxi Daddy took her hand in his and said, "Listen, angel, the unpleasant fact is we can't go through life without sometimes being with people we don't much care for, for such is the kingdom of Heaven, God damn it."

But please come for me *early,* she begged. "And you won't want to leave," he said. That was always the way of it, Daddy said, the party you don't want to go to is always the party you don't want to leave.

But Daddy had not been right this time. It was deadly. With gifts for everyone. She received a police whistle. "How or yew, moi dear?" the mother said. A few boys danced reluctantly with her and one of them asked had she gone to Miss Parsons' School on Seventy-fifth Street and when she said yes she had, said his dead sister had gone there too. It was, as she had predicted, un-special and she had actually heard some old woman say it was so nice to see "the young people" having a good time.

She got on her high horse and stayed on it until they said (thank God) her father had come.

Not until they were almost home in the cab had she discovered she must have taken the wrong raincoat when she found a pack of Virginia Rounds cigarettes in a pocket. So they had to turn around and go back. The party was just about over and they were told a girl named Lacey Edwards had Tess's coat and given an address on Sutton Place. It turned out to be in a pretty row of two-story houses facing the river.

After a conversation at the door and handing over the coat, Daddy

34

came back to the taxi. "Where's my coat?" "She said wouldn't we come in a minute?" "Oh, what for?" "Just to come in. I think we might," Daddy said and paid the taxi, seemed rather pleased to be asked, and it was odd because ordinarily Daddy shunned strangers like the plague, could be fierce with strangers, warding them off with his great hearty charm.

In the hallway of the little house stood this creature, pale, iridescent. "I'm Zina Edwards," she said and extended a hand to Tess. "And did you have as bloody a time as Lacey did?" She was a dragonfly, Tess thought. She was wearing this wonderful shimmering floating something that was the exact color of flies' wings in sunlight; she had a long pointed face and nose and strange thick black hair which flew out everywhere in curls and knots and she was strikingly attractive in an ugly way. They followed her into a low-ceilinged room with a black-and-white-tiled floor and Tiffany lamps and great tall ferns and plants, lots of pale yellow silk furniture, on which sat and sprawled a mixed bag of people, including a stunning-looking black man who was in the middle of quoting something in impeccable (it sounded) German and obviously everyone else could follow it because they nodded at each word and made noises of approval; then a very lined-faced woman said, "But, Gregory, in English for the likes of me," and the black man said, " 'O my brethren! With whom lieth the greatest danger to the whole human future? Is it not with the *good* and the *just?*' " "Amen," the woman said. Nobody turned around to greet them and Zina Edwards poured a dark liquid into a stirrup cup and said, "Have some Black Velvet, Mr. Adams." Found ginger ale for Tess and called out (she had a low voice which exactly suited her), "Lacey, some extraordinarily nice people have brought your coat."

Lacey was small with black hair like her mother's and quick beady eyes that took the whole of Tess in at a glance, June Allyson dress and all, as she said "Hello." Lacey was wearing a party dress also but it seemed at least two years ahead of her, like an evening dress made for a midget; it even had a cutaway back and was very grown up. It was brown velvet and she had on little brown velvet shoes. "Come

35

upstairs," Lacey said and darted upstairs, with Tess following. Her bedroom was violently untidy and had a French poster on the wall depicting what seemed to be a rape at a ball. Lacey lit a Virginia Rounds and indicated that Tess sit on the bed, which she did, feeling curiously prim clutching her ginger ale. "Better here," she said, "than downstairs with those fakes. Ugh, they're all so fakey. My mother doesn't know any ordinary *people;* it's *pathetic* is what it is. Do you go to Dalton?"

"Yes," Tess said. "How did you guess?"

"You have the look," Lacey said as if with pity.

"Where do *you* go?"

"I just got canned from Chapin. You've no idea how insular they are there, worse than Dalton, I imagine. So I'm just coasting along until I can get into the School of Professional Arts. It's terrifically difficult to get into."

"Are you going to be an actress?"

"Do you have a lipstick?"

"Yes," Tess said.

Lacey borrowed her lipstick and applied it lavishly without looking in a mirror; the first of all the things Lacey would borrow over the years. For she appeared to have a need to borrow things, perhaps a need for establishing herself, of making herself securely felt, and in the way that some aquatic mammals must rise to the surface every now and then to breathe, so Lacey borrowed little things. Do you have a Kleenex? Lend me your comb, will you? Do you have a pencil? Give me a dollar for the doorman.

"What does your father do?" Lacey asked.

"He imports Scotch whisky."

"Oh."

"A very expensive brand," Tess said unnecessarily.

"I don't think that'll please my mother."

"Why?"

"It's too ordinary."

"We only stopped in for a minute for a drink," Tess said and stood up to go.

36

"Oh, sit down. They'll be hours yet."

But feeling a twinge of pique at her father's being "ordinary" and finding no way in cold blood of saying that well, her mother was Amelia Van Hoorens, the cellist, Tess remained standing.

"What does *your* father do?" she asked.

"I don't have a father."

Dead? Divorced? "I'm sorry."

"I mean, of course I *have* a father. Oh, I have a father. But only in the procreative sense."

"I see," Tess said and was too polite to pursue it.

"If I was to tell you who my father is," Lacey said, "you would go right *through* that floor. You see, my father is super famous. I mean, not ordinary run-of-the-mill famous but super super *world-*celebrated famous. I mean, so it would block the street outside if it got around he was in the house."

"Whew," Tess said inadequately. Inadequate was what she felt in the presence of this alarming girl in her brown velvet dress and her cigarettes and her world-famous father.

She waited but Lacey seemed to have dropped the subject.

"And *does* he come here?" she asked.

"Oh, no, he's never been here," Lacey said. "For various reasons I can't divulge to you, I have never seen him."

"Oh."

"In person, that is."

"Oh."

"Every New Year's Eve without failing—without *failing*—he calls my mother up just before midnight from wherever he is in the world to say—he always says just thing one thing and then hangs up—'Happy New Year 1931.'"

"Why 1931?"

"That was the night I was conceived, that New Year's Eve."

"Oh."

"And it was some kind of peak for him, he told a reporter once —not my conception but that year, and after that, he said, everything began to go wrong."

"Oh." Who on God's earth could he be? Movie star? Senator? Who was the President in 1931?

"Once she let me listen in."

"Your *mother* did?"

"No, Madame Chiang Kai-shek." Lacey closed her eyes a moment and acted weary, weary to death with people who asked inane questions, and "I'm sorry," Tess said quickly, not to irritate this exotic creature.

After a long look that implied much about noblesse oblige, Lacey went on, "Well, it was very exciting, very emotional for me, because I was going to hear his voice for the first time and he was calling from Caracas and there was all this long-distance crackling and beeping and then he said hello and hello, my mother said and used his first name and he said hello, Zina, precious and there was this pause and he gave this terrible sigh—you could hear it all the way from Caracas —and then he said in this low low sad voice that made you want to cry, he said well, baby, happy New Year 1931."

"Good night," Tess said; it was the nearest she could then get to blasphemy. "Good *night.*"

"Yes," Lacey said. "You might say that."

"Was—did your mother have a—I mean, was she married to somebody else when—"

"Technically my mother was Mrs. Horace Quested Edwards III but she had left him long before she met *my* father."

My father. Even her tone elevated him to eminence, as though she were a royal bastard who was entitled to use the crest (but upside down) on her underwear; she was a fraction too conceited about it. And (Tess rankled slightly in the presence of this fifteen-year-old grande dame) if her Daddy was too "ordinary" to please Lacey's mother, then Lacey's mother was certainly going to be a bit too racy for Daddy.

Daddy got drunk often and sang and danced wildly during these sprees, swept women into deep embraces, led the way to the midnight swim, embarrassed the kitchen help by appearing suddenly in their midst to speak an emotional toast to them, got off the Super

Chief at Needles on a whim to see what it was like, leaving Mother and baggage on the train, and was lost for four days—was sometimes known as Wild Johnny Adams—yet Daddy had in him a little nodule of puritanism. Daddy might, just might, be shocked about Lacey's being a bastard and being so cocky about it.

"I daresay of course you know who my ma is," Lacey said.

"Mrs. Edwards?"

"How old are you?"

"Sixteen and a half."

"You act more like fourteen."

"Well . . ."

"She's the Zina of the Bergdorf ads," Lacey said and then, *"Surely* you look at the Bergdorf ads."

"Not really very often."

"No," Lacey said, looking at Tess's dress, "probably not. Well, she's the artist that does all those long swooping women in dresses and scarves and jewelry and so on. She's the 'Zina' you always see at the bottom."

"Oh."

"Have you read *The Fountainhead* by Ayn Rand?"

"No."

It led to—not a discussion; Tess said nothing—a varicolored report on what Lacey thought were currently the things to read and to see at the movies; Tess had not heard of any of the books nor seen ads for any of the movies, all of which seemed to be playing uptown at the Thalia or downtown at the Art in the Village. She was considering how intellectually undernourished she must seem to Lacey, how ovine, when Lacey said, surprisingly taking her hand, "Let's go downstairs and snub those fakes; let's go downstairs and be *terrifically* haughty."

On the narrow staircase she pulled Tess toward her and whispered, "The reason she has these fakes around her is she's so frightened of being ordinary."

But to their surprise the party had emptied out, except for the handsome black talking in a corner to a woman dressed all in fringe who kept shivering and pulling her fringe around her as if she was thrilled or cold.

Zina Edwards and Daddy sat on a sofa. Daddy's back was to Tess but she could tell by his gestures he'd had several drinks in the short time she'd been upstairs and that he was enjoying himself. He was talking expansively and gesturing with his hands, drink in one, cigarette in the other, and Zina seemed either spellbound or on the point of sleep, one hand with its amethyst ring touching her chin, her eyes slitted. When Tess and Lacey came toward them, neither of them moved and Lacey raised her eyebrows in a display of boredom and then said to her mother, "Can I have a little vermouth on the rocks?"

"Well," Daddy said, interrupted, turning to Tess. He was flushed. "And is this Lucy?"

"Lacey," Lacey said and looked Daddy up and down. "Can I have one of your cigarettes?"

And Daddy looked surprised but Zina said, "Oh, she smokes, a little."

"You're very grown up, aren't you?" Daddy said and flicked his lighter for Lacey.

"Well, Tess," Daddy said, "you have made us stay too long."

And in the hall Daddy said to Zina, "Thank you" and held on to her hand too long.

"For what?" Zina asked. The way she was looking at Daddy didn't intimate he was too ordinary for her.

"Most gracious beautiful lady," Daddy said and Tess knew the voice. It was the bubbly voice as if his glottis were all soda water; it was unmistakably the voice Daddy had when he was a little drunk and sexy.

Then, *"Taxi,"* Daddy roared, charging down the steps.

It was all over so fast that Tess had no time to frame any suitable words to Lacey, like maybe we can meet, or could I call you? Though Lacey must be taken up with a superfluity of friends. But looking back through the cab window she saw Lacey was still standing in the front door and that she seemed to have deflated, shrunk, and in the mournful blue street light shining on her she looked like a skinny

40

child abandoned and dressed by the Salvation Army in somebody's old evening gown.

" 'Oh, the more we are together, together, together,' " Daddy sang, his arm squeezing Tess's shoulder, " 'the happier we'll be.' "

It was funny. Usually she would have snuggled close to him and sung too but here she was staring out at the street lights flashing by and almost about to say, "Oh, don't be so infantile; why must you always act infantile when someone takes notice of you?"

Mama came into the hall in an alarmed way. "Well, it must have been a good party. You stayed an *aw*fully long time. I just was beginning to get a bit frantic, it's been so long."

"Well—" Tess began to explain about the wrong coats and where they had been all this time but "Errrummph," Daddy said, skirting around behind Mama and giving Tess a wink. So they were not to tell.

"Who was there?" Mama asked, following Tess into her room. "Was it fun, darling? Did anyone compliment you on your dress?"

At the Metropolitan, Daddy yanked her arm and said, "Let's go this way and see the early Greeks and Romans."

She never had much enthusiasm for the Greeks and Romans; such a tedious lot of look-alikes and all with something missing. The whole wing reminded her of petrified calamity, as though she had arrived in Pompeii a week after the eruption: the sightless eyes, missing hands and legs, the huge torsos and buttocks unattached to the rest of a body, noses eaten away. She had wanted to go upstairs right away and find her Bronzino boy, the one in black velvet with the cast in his eye, but Daddy said let's go this way and see the early Greeks and Romans. He liked very definite things, Rubenses and Tintorettos. Everything about today was a bit unexpected, even lunch (out of the blue, get your coat on and we'll go to the Stanhope for lunch and have oysters first), and then coming out of the Stanhope he said oh, why don't we drop into the Metropolitan as it's right here. "Ah," he said from time to time. "Eleventh century B.C." "Mmmm. From near Crete, sixth century. How about that, Tiz?"

Behind a huge torso were Zina Edwards and Lacey.

He took a step backward and made a comic gesture of covering his eyes and said, "I am seeing things."

Zina was all in black as if in deep mourning. "Mr. Adams, I'll be bound," she said in her throaty voice. Lacey was in dirty blue jeans and a leather coat. She was wearing dark sunglasses, perhaps to safeguard her from any glimpse of art.

"Hello, Tess," Lacey said. You could not tell whether she was amused or annoyed at being a ploy.

Tess was annoyed beyond words at being a ploy and cross with herself for thinking he had wanted to have lunch with her *alone.*

But like bored parents, she and Lacey went along with the two middle-aged plotters. You couldn't believe it, the way Zina and her father were laying it on with a trowel.

"I said to Lacey I've got an urge to see . . ."

"We were just lunching across at the Stanhope, so I said . . ."

"Coincidence . . ."

"I surely must tell you how much I enjoyed myself the other evening . . ."

". . . rush off like that."

So they walked ahead, as mannered as peacocks, stepping this way and that; their politeness was almost sensual.

"And this," Zina said as if she owned it, "is a crouching Aphrodite."

"Goddess of love, beauty and fertility," Daddy read and very lightly touched Zina.

"Herakles." Zina pointed.

"Do you have any gum or a mint or a Life Saver?" Lacey asked.

"No," Tess said. She was allowing them to see she was annoyed at being used. She barely looked at anything and when Zina said, "You see, sometimes these were put in the caves as votive offerings," she said, "Oh, *really?* Wonders will never cease," and later on when Zina, who seemed to know everything about Grecian art (more than one wanted to hear), said that this was Sostratos holding his strigil, she grabbed it rudely and said, "Holding his *what?*"

"Latin for a scraper," Zina said and Daddy put an arm around Tess a moment and said sweetly, "Darling, don't be a grudge."

"When he called up," Lacey said as they lingered behind, "*she* said come to the house but he wanted to arrange it so we ran into each other and you know, I think she was intrigued, he's so square and sincere. I think she's intrigued after all those fakes to meet someone like him. She pretended to laugh it off. 'Can you believe the old square?' she said and then she went upstairs and took off all her makeup and put on fresh."

"Oh, she *told* you he called."

"Oh, she tells me everything," Lacey said.

"Why did she bring you along?"

"She didn't bring me along. She couldn't bring me to the table if I didn't want. I came to see you."

Well. Tess was flattered. Lacey liked her, then. But it didn't excuse Daddy's behavior.

"She's *interested,* all right," Lacey said.

"Well, I hope she doesn't get too serious about him because it never lasts," Tess said and glared at a god sprawled drunkenly beside her, over whose genitals a fly was walking.

Her father was a born enchanter and women, especially his own age, frequently mistook his gift for easy sexual raillery for intent. Often he had to retreat rapidly into protocol; Miss Brian at the office was versed in getting rid of women with poignant, passionate voices asking when, *when* would Mr. Adams be back? Some grew so desperate they phoned the apartment and then it was Mrs. Adams who dealt with them; they didn't get anywhere with Amelia Van Hoorens Adams. Her vagueness was totally sincere; her distraction was fathomless; it would have been within the bounds of possibility for Amelia to ask *which* Mr. Adams?

What was different about this time, then?

"Tea?"

Zina did everything with concentrated clarity; she outlined the idea of tea. "Come home with us and have tea," she had suggested suddenly in the European wing just as they had all had about enough art. But the way she said "tea" made it sound voluptuous, even forbidden. She brewed it in a silver pot. "Tea?" she suggested, and the word was dark amber. "Raisin toast?" she said, surprised at even thinking of it but suddenly making raisin toast so delicious the mouth watered.

So it seemed to be with everything she said and did; as though it had occurred to her only that moment. Tea? Raisin toast? As though she made up her life as she went along. She would be equally capable of saying Europe? Love? She would be delighted at the thought.

Shall we have a fire?

So she must have said to this World Celebrity, "Shall we have a child?" So she said to John Adams, "Shall we have an affair?" not in those words but tasting, testing. "Who will win the pennant this year, do you think?" "Is Truman any good, do you think?" "Do you believe all this flying saucer stuff?" Do you feel about me as I feel about you?

And Daddy's foot was going up and down like a cat's tail. He leaned toward her, elbow on one knee, cup in hand, and prefaced everything with "Let me ask you this . . ." or "Presuming, like me, you are . . ." and her father's being formal this way with Zina was a dead giveaway, Tess thought. What was different about this time opposed to other ladies was that Daddy was for once not in the lead but being led and liking it.

And Zina Edwards being about the sexiest woman Tess had ever come across; also something about her hands being large and ugly (the only ungainly things about her): they were the hands of a Swedish masseuse and something about them suggested sex.

The twilight became thick and dark blue and they sat playing their game of shall we have an affair until (perhaps at some secret signal) Lacey said, "Tess, you want to come and see *Les Enfants du Paradis* with me?" Oh, fine, she said, sometime this week? "No, now," Lacey said. Oh, not *now,* she exclaimed.

"Run *along,* darling," Daddy said. "Here's five dollars so you can get a cab home."

44

"A drink?" Zina was saying as the girls put on their coats.

Tess found *Les Enfants du Paradis* long and difficult to follow and she could not keep her mind on the subtitles.

It was as if she were a child again and somebody had let go of her hand in a crowded store and simply walked off and left her. She felt strange and kept her bedroom door closed so he would knock on it and then felt angry and hurt when she heard him go by and he didn't. He seemed so preoccupied now.

She got out his letters to her when she had been in boarding school.

Dearest Thing: Well, we got home from driving you up there and the apartment seems so empty and big without you. I just looked into your room and lo and behold there was nothing there but a big yellow moon looking in the window and a big lonely Daddy.

Darling Tizzie: Do I miss you? Well, did I ever tell you about the Terrible Nasty Cruel Dentist of Tarrytown? Well, when I was a boy we had this dentist Dr. Ringgold (Dr. Ring*worm* would have been more appropriate) and he used to say to me, "Johnnie, I have to drill and because of where the nerve is I can't give you a needle first," and then he'd drill right on the nerve and keep on doing it and watching me to see how soon I'd yell bloody murder and so I'd hold onto the arms of the chair till I guess I almost tore them off so as not to groan even and that's the way I'm trying not to cry over missing my girl.

Dear Miss Adams: I am writing to ask you a great personal favor. At considerable trouble and expense I have negotiated the purchase of two third-row orchestra seats for the new Rogers [spelled wrong] and Hammerstein show for Thanksgiving Day night, which week I am reliably informed you are to be spending in New York. I am writing to ask most humbly whether you would consider being my date for that evening (if you are not already inundated with invitations) and would dine with me first at the Edwardian Room at the Plaza Hotel. Your sincere and devoted admirer, John Purvis Adams.

Now, Tess, I don't know all the facts concerning your argument with this girl Sheila Hipple (?) (I can't read your writing—you *seemed* to be very tensed up when you wrote) but it seems clear you lost the battle to her. Now the important thing is not whether you won or lost a silly argument with this girl but that (it seems to me) you were lacking conviction and borrowing other people's ideas on the subject and so she beat you and you got mad. Darling, *never* borrow other people's opinions without first trying them out or at least thinking them through in relation to yourself. It always leaves you open to unexpected gaps and contradictions that not only lose you the argument but shake your self-confidence. Besides, it's lazy. For God's sake have your *own* opinion and stick to it. I love you. Daddy.

> Where's my little Tessie-pie?
> Like a diamond in the sky.
> Is she playing hide and seek?
> Not a word since Monday week.

It reminded her of her getting sick, perhaps deliberately, in that hateful school with its bleak gray rooms and windy corridors and how, when she got word out to him, he came and stormed at the headmistress and the school doctor when they started in about rules and he shouted rules be damned, this is my child, and dramatically scooped her up out of bed and in her nightie carried her downstairs in his arms and right through the main hall where the girls were assembled for supper, carried her, with her head nestling in his chest, to the car.

But now when she closed her bedroom door as a hint he didn't respond; met her in the hall and looked at her in mild surprise and said, "Hi, darling" or "Hello, my Tiz," vaguely. Now in the incredibly short time since Zina Edwards, her father was simply not her father any more. And on weekends when they went as usual up to the big Bedford house he seemed not to enjoy it; blustered around the hills like a gale and gave himself away constantly by saying things like oh, I don't think we ought to light a fire because I must be back in town early this evening. She watched him burning with impatience to get to Zina. Sometimes now, incredibly, they didn't go up to the Bedford house for the weekend; he was kept in town on inexplicable business.

She watched him steeped in happiness (or was it melancholy and if so were the two emotions alike?), sitting at the dinner table drumming his fingers on the tablecloth and gazing at something a thousand miles away from which he occasionally came back with an effort. Oh? he said or Uh-huh, or "How did it go today?" he asked her, standing at the window with his back to her and watching the snow swirl around the Seventy-first Street lights.

Why, she said, she got an A in this, a B in that, she couldn't *begin* to tell him how awful was her algebra and the algebra teacher unqualified to teach and a sadist to boot was her opinion. And "Aha" and "Uh-huh," Daddy said.

"Well," she said, "and then I slipped in the corridor between geography and French and the wound was very very deep and became infected so they had to amputate my leg."

"Uh-huh. That's nice, sweetness."

She threw a book. Missed him. "Don't bother to listen," she screamed.

"I am. I *am*. I will. I *will*."

Later, "Sorry, darling angel. Forgive? Daddy's got a business problem on his mind." Big kiss on her neck. "Forgive?"

"Forgive."

She was being forced against her will into corruption. She not only noted down his lies; she spied, she eavesdropped. Came home and, taking off her snow boots, heard him talking on the extension phone that was in the little room they used for coats and umbrellas when guests came. Behind the closed living room door, her mother, who was getting ready for a recital, was practicing and the deep cello notes wept and mourned under what Daddy was saying. Saying, "But *do* you, *do* you?" saying, "In my whole *life*," as Tess flattened herself against the wall, the way she had seen eavesdroppers do in movies, hands spread against the wall, and heard him say, "My darling, darling woman, it is hell; it is no easier for *me* going about my business all day, I can tell you." On and on he went, pouring out his ecstasy or unhappiness while all the time behind the closed living room door Mama accompanied him on her cello. The low, sad voice of the cello soared and throbbed behind Daddy's voice saying, "Because I've not been affected this way in my life before, not ever," and behind Daddy choking up and whispering, "Oh, darling woman, darling woman." All the time Tess flattened against the wall listening.

How sneaky rotten he was making her feel, dirty, to snoop around their love affair. Was that what was making her angry? She was livid with anger. She wished him dead. No, that was going too far. She wanted him *always*. She wished him . . . well, *ill*. Ill and with something infectious like, say, yellow fever and having had scarlet fever when she was nine she was immune probably and would be the only one able to nurse him. Day and night she wrung out wet cloths to cool his fever, sat by his bed and fanned him through the nights, and everyone would say you *must* rest, you *must* get some sleep, Tess, no human being can go as you have gone sixty-eight hours without lying down for a few winks of sleep, without once changing your clothes, taking off your shoes. She would shoo them all away, fanning him, fanning him, until the fever broke, the crisis passed and he fell into a restful sleep and then opening his eyes would see her and reach out for . . .

"H'lo?"

"It's Lacey."

"Hi."

"Listen, I'm being shipped away."

"Where to?"

"France."

"What *for?* Why?"

"Well, you know *why*. Ostensibly I'm going to live with a French family for four months so as to learn to speak fluently."

"French?"

"No, Chinese."

"All of a sudden like this?"

"*Oui.* I said to her, 'Oh, I see through you, Mother, so don't add to the hypocrisy by pretending it's only to give me decent French.' Well, they can't just keep on meeting in the Stanhope bar and then going to some place he has, some place way up in the Nineties; this friend loans him the apartment. Well, they're getting so edgy; you can't blame them, it's pretty sordid and *she* isn't used to that kind of arrangement. . . . Hello?"

"Yes, I'm here."

"Thought we'd been disconnected. Anyway, I said to her, 'It's like the way you had *me.* Not for the sake of having *me* but for the sake of my being *his.* You know. Such-and-such, whose name I'm not allowed to tell you. I told her she's been trading on me all my life, on my being that person's child just so she can think how marvelous it was having had *him.* Oh, I tell you, *les parents sont merdes.*"

So Lacey left and Daddy gave Mama a pearl-and-sapphire ring. Mama took it in a somewhat hazy way and said, "Well, Jack, well, *Jack,* this is very sweet and you really shouldn't have been so extravagant just at the time when you have all the expenses of my recital. . . ." Then she put on the ring and stared at it without enthusiasm and with perhaps the look of a girl who has become engaged, but reluctantly, to the only possible suitor; Mama had the look of a sad girl who has had to settle for the best she can get, which of course had not been true in Mama's case. She eyed the ring with curious resignation and then Tess caught Daddy's eye and he had the cruelty and incredible insolence to twinkle at her so she choked down bread so as not to scream out that the ring was just nothing but guilt because all afternoon probably he had been in bed with Zina.

But then when (and he was in a hugely jovial mood) he said, "My God, it burns me up, this thing with General Motors trying to get away with something like that; why, it's pure out-and-out lies and corruption—"

"Good *Christ,*" Tess exploded, "listen to who's being moral."

And "Leave the table," Daddy said. "I will not have you using language like that at the table or *anywhere.* Hear me?"

"I hear you," she said, getting up and going out.

"Never. Do you hear me?" he shouted. "You will stay in your room until you are ready to apologize *properly* to me."

Funnily, one of the rare times Mama came to console her.

"Dear," Mama said, "is something wrong? Tess, I think it's these continual bad grades that's upsetting you."

Oh, Mama, she wanted to say, I feel betrayed.

"Or is it something troubling you, dear?"

"No, he just makes me sick."

"But *why?* Is it because we're not going to Bermuda for Christmas?"

"No."

"But, Tess, you are so *violent* for you and he's perfectly right about profanity like that. Profanity is not attractive, dear, under any circumstances. But what on *earth* is wrong, Tess? I wish you'd tell me."

She might then and there have poured it all out to Mama if she could have brought herself to be such a Judas, giving Daddy away, but at the moment she looked into her mother's concerned eyes, the concerned eyes wandered over her shoulder; Mama leaned toward her but as she waited for the expected caress, Mama reached out and took hold of one of the drapes behind her and peered at it and said, "Do you know your draperies are upside down? I thought these things were little garlands but they're sea horses upside down. Can you imagine? And we never noticed. Well, I just can't get *over* Altman's doing a thing like that."

Oh, ho, ho, ho, Mama laughed, going out, ho, ho, ho. Mama's rare laugh (usually hidden with a hand over her mouth; excuse her for laughing) and What? What? Daddy's voice said irritably. "Oh, Jack, we're laughing because for two years it must be now, Tessie's draperies have been hanging upside down. Oh, isn't it *amusing?* Poor Tess with upside-down draperies and we have never even *noticed.*"

Once a year Mama gave a recital. This was something Daddy gave Mama. About a month before, it was advertised on the concert page of the Sunday *New York Times* among the glut of recitals: *"Amelia Van Hoorens, Cellist.* Carnegie Recital Hall, Tuesday December 8 at 8:30 sharp. Works by Reger, Bach, Korda, Bloch. $4 $3 $2." The small auditorium was always about two-thirds filled. It was not known by Mama (one imagined) that Daddy paid for these seats, telephoned and gently prodded, blackmailed. Friends and acquaintances came in evening dress and scattered around were the people *they* knew who were musical but poor and endured in rooming houses and walk-ups, waiting for *any* treat to be thrown them like a bone. Programs were printed with a photograph of Mama on the front and Avery Marchbanks was engaged as accompanist and rehearsed at home with Mama for a month or so every day and followed her onto the platform as if he had gangrenous feet and stood diffidently aside while Mama made three sharp bows. The applause from the friends was too loud and gratuitous; it was as if Mama were Pablo Casals. It was led by Daddy and went on for easily a minute and a half when she appeared and after each number. Then Mama sat and tuned up and waited while the coughs and squeakings of the hard Austrian chairs subsided. Then a strange thing happened. Mama became beautiful. Mama's long thin apologetic face became lovely and the first mourning resonant notes took Mama away on some dream she had once had.

Mama should have gone to Leipzig or Salzburg, they had said when she graduated from Juilliard. But Mama married big John Adams, who could not carry a tune in his head, not "Yankee Doodle" even. So it was rather sweet to watch Daddy out of the corner of one's eye, leg crossed over leg in the evening trousers with the satin stripe; Daddy perspiring a little in starched evening shirt, beautifully shaven and lotioned and combed and pink and with his glasses on so he could go through his procedure of looking at the program, then settling back, program in hand, and adopting the intense look of the music lover. And when the last soulful note died away and Mama remained as still as though she had died too in that final second of parting with the dream, head down, hand and bow still on the string, the accompanist with one hand hovering over the

51

dying piano note, there was absolute silence until Daddy (always) grunted *Unnk*. *Unnk*, Daddy grunted, which translated into "Beautiful beyond words," so the friends grunted too, turning this and that way to each other, *Unnk, Unnk,* then burst into applause while Mama came back, startled, looked abruptly at her cello as though she had just found it in a bus.

And Mama's mama, Grandma Van Hoorens, had been too "swacked" (Aunt Rosine's word) to come to the wedding and severe bronchitis was given as the excuse. Everybody in that part of Pennsylvania knew that Mrs. Van Hoorens drank and that that was why to this day Mama never took a drink, not once in her life, even on New Year's Eve or at her wedding, and so on top of everything else they seemed not to have in common, that she would choose the son of one of the (before prohibition) biggest importers of Scotch whisky in the country was considered whimsical of her. Like her campaigns against the hunting of deer and pheasant in what was hunting country. All Tess knew about Mama's youth and how she met Daddy and all about Juilliard and so forth came from Mama's older sister Rosine, who told it with seeming enthusiasm for everything Mama had ever done, told it with relish, all the time running her little tongue over her little front teeth like a kitten and giving little twitches and smoking fiercely one cigarette after another. So *gifted,* Aunt Rosine said, so *disciplined,* so *talented.* It was clear, Tess thought, Aunt Rosine detested Mama.

And the year Mama graduated from Juilliard and they said she ought to study in Leipzig she came down home for Christmas–New Year's and it was that Christmas Jack Adams came to stay with the Bunces and caused such a flustering of wild hopes among girls and mothers in Coleville with his good looks and the fact that he was a "catch" and "Your father was then—still is, to a degree—the hand-somest man I ever saw and perhaps the most charming," Aunt Rosine said, smoking fiercely, her little eyes narrowed with amusement at life's little ironies because "all the girls were falling *over* themselves to get his attention at the parties and lunches and the *funny* thing was—ha, ha, ha, oh, I have to *laugh* when I think about it—

he had set his cap for *me*. Oh, ho, ho, ho, ho, and *I* wasn't interested and every pretty girl in Coleville was literally at his feet and then who should come along and carry him off? My baby sister. My little baby birdlike sister, Amelia." Aunt Rosine snickered and rocked with amusement, hugging herself with her thin arms. "Just like *that*. Oh, nobody could believe their eyes. Oh, what a *yock* it was."

Well, now, but the only sad thing, the fly in the ointment was the wicked waste of Mama's talent, said Aunt Rosine. Mama was terrifically talented and would have had a *world* career and gave it all up to marry this big jolly fun-loving Jack Adams. Oh, well, she must have *wanted* to. But what waste.

"Wicked," Aunt Rosine said. "Just criminal. She was so gifted. Well, I guess she never regretted it. . . ."

Except . . .

She did that strange thing in Milan. "I don't think I ever told you this, did I?" Aunt Rosine asked. About the time Aunt Rosine went to Europe with Mama and Daddy when Tess was about six, leaving her with her Aunt Gretchen? Aunt Rosine said she hadn't *wanted* to go but Daddy *insisted,* just about laid down the *law* she come along because she'd had a "silly little bit of a" nervous breakdown and besides, "Jack and I always got along well and I was someone he could have a drink and a yock or two with whereas Mama didn't drink and always constantly wanted to be going to *concerts."* It seemed Aunt Rosine and Daddy sat in a lot of bars and had a lot of yocks. Well, then, Mama disappeared in Milan. On the day they were leaving for Zermatt. At first they thought she'd just gone out to buy soap or some last-minute thing. But she didn't come back. They had to let one train go, then another. They were frantic. They went around searching in sidewalk cafés and shops. By evening they had the concierge call the police and hospitals to see if an American woman had been in an accident. Then just as they had been trying to reach the American vice-consul at his home, Mama had walked calmly into the hotel lobby eating a *gelato* and just as cool and with no explanation while Daddy, practically incoherent with the anger of relief, raged and raged at her (not caring about the Italian stares) about just what the hell did she think she was doing frightening him out of his wits to say nothing of what she had done to poor Rosine, who was just getting over a nervous breakdown, just why, and what in the name of God could possess her to do a thing like that? And after a long while of only saying I'm sorry, Jack, I'm sorry and All I can say is I'm *sorry*, Mama had finally said, "Well, I wanted to see just for a few hours what it might have been like having a life of my own."

Aunt Rosine's eyebrows said madness, suicide. Said perhaps being married to John Adams . . .

She presented one of the adages she seemed to think were her own and brand new, they pleased her so.

Well, Tess, people make their beds.

Aunt Rosine died with a fish bone in her throat in a restaurant in New Orleans, a city she had not liked to begin with, and Mama had never again done anything unusual.

Never went off anywhere except into music, like now, where she was away in the Korda sonata.

Her arms moving over the cello in a way that lovers pass their hands over each other, Tess imagined, and became aware Daddy was staring away to the right and that across the aisle Zina Edwards had crept in late and all in silver with a silver turban (too gala for little Carnegie Recital Hall) and had turned her face to Daddy and though Tess could not see *his* face she could see on Zina's face that what was being said between them had to be real and tremendous, so much so that it must sting their hearts like breathing in subzero weather, and it flashed through Tess that it was sincere and desperate and hungry and that she might go through life and miss having a love like that, it was probably rare, and the thought rushed through her like fire, making her so frightened and angry that when she turned her face toward the platform she saw three Mamas playing three cellos.

"I simply cut her dead."
"Very rude of you. I noticed."

They were having it out. She was wild.

"Asking her to Mama's recital . . ."

"Tizzie . . ."

"Well, I just think it was an insult to Mama."

"Tiz-zie."

"And in front of all Mama's friends."

"Tiz-*zie.*"

"And paying court to her while my poor mother is—"

"Now stop," he said and held up a finger. "Just stop pretending all this is out of concern for your mother."

"I happen to *have* concern for my mother."

"Then I wish you'd show her more of it."

"Oh, that's terrific coming from *you.*"

"What I mean is, don't fly into a tantrum with me and pretend it's because you're upset for Mama. I won't listen to a lot of high and mighty piffle about Mama. You are upset over me and Mrs. Edwards. Right?"

"Oh, I couldn't care less what you do, Father."

"Now listen, *listen,* sweetheart, I won't take this guff from you. You are upset about me and Mrs. Edwards, right?"

"It's none of my business what you and Mrs. Edwards do."

"That's correct. Nevertheless you're upset, right? Answer me."

"Well, I think it's pretty cheap of you."

"Yes, I've known you do but thank you for answering me straight because this concerns you and me directly in what upsets *you.* Now would it make you feel any better if I *told* Mama?"

"I don't know."

"Would it make Mama feel better if she knew?"

"I don't know. I don't suppose it would."

"What good would it do?"

"Oh, you make it sound perfectly *all right* to go on doing this; you make it sound just fine."

"You want me to grovel around, darling, and say a lot of—a lot of contrite lies to you. I won't do that, baby, because I'm not sorry."

"No, you can't do wrong."

"Tessie, Tessie, I'm as wrong as hell and selfish and deceitful, and since you seem to want to know, I aim to go *on* being."

"Oh, I'm sure you do."

"With no excuses, understand?"

"Perfectly."

"Is that what you wanted to know?"

"Partly. I thought you'd say something like that. Uh-huh."

"I won't *stress* the fact I'd much prefer not to have this out, as you put it."

"I'm sure you wouldn't. Anyway, I haven't got anything more to say, so—"

"Wait, please."

"I don't want to hear anything you have to say about it at all, period—at *all.*"

"—put it this way and do me the courtesy, please, to sit down again until I've finished, Tess."

"Certainly."

"Oh, God. Let me put it this way, then. Would you mind looking at me just for a minute? Thank you. Let me just say this, baby, and I'll never say another thing about it. If I had to live my life over and if this . . . thing came into my life again I would do it all over again. But it has not and never will affect my love for you. You are my blessed darling girl and nothing can alter that but it's such a miraculous thing that's happened to me, you couldn't know what it's like to have someone come into your life at a time when you think nothing more will happen and that maybe you've missed the best thing and I'm sorry if it's upset you but it's not like anything I've had before in my whole life, not even with Mama, who I love, whether you want to believe it or not, in a whole different way. You see, this is the thing I never thought *could* happen. So I'm being completely frank with you, dearest, and I only ask you to *try* to be just a little understanding. Only because it may happen to you one day. I *hope* it happens to you."

"Finished, Father?"

*　*　*

"Now, my dear, here's someone to see you," the matron said, swishing suddenly around the corner into the ugly little visitors' room at Biding where Tess and Lacey were sitting.

"Here's someone who wants to say something to you," the matron said with her hard smiles raining down on Tess. The matron stepped into the hall and clapped her hands twice. "Doyle," she said. "Come."

Doyle? Tess didn't know any Doyle. It was rather alarming the way they forced people on you and best to be on your guard because it was possible nowadays for all kinds of unpleasant tricks to be played on "old" people in the guise of treats. There were frequently people who were "called for" earlier than expected and told they were going to some nice place, some old-fashioned picnic arranged, or to hear the taped band concert, only to discover themselves on the bus to the death chamber, not even having been allowed to say good-bye to their family.

"Big-ass," Lacey muttered at the matron, who brought in a stocky fiftyish woman in uniform, with faded red hair.

"Here's Doyle," the matron said. "Wants to say hello to you." The matron squished out.

"I'm Eunice," Doyle said.

"Oh, *Eunice,* I didn't recognize you. What a lot of years, my dear." Eunice had worked for Tess and Elton. Had come to them when she was about fifteen to do kitchen help. She had helped serve at the bigger parties and laundered. Her way with a blouse had been that of an angel. "Oh, Eunice," Tess would say, admiring the work of art. "The way you do a blouse, I almost hate to wear it."

Now the sight of Eunice prompted emotions in her. Strangely the laundress, part-time help scarcely remembered, touched her on a raw place. She shook Eunice's red paw. "Oh, Eunice," she said, "how nice to see you. Oh, do you remember the parties? Do you

57

remember the little yellow roses you used to help me pick for the table?"

"I saw you come in," Eunice said. She had developed the colorless voice of these institutionalized times. When domestic service had been abolished, she had gone to a school for social behavior work and had graduated (she proudly told Tess) as something which was called, without a trace of irony, a Servant.

"You were very kind to me," Eunice said.

"Oh, Eunice, you were like one of the family."

"I remember you giving me dresses and things."

"Oh, Eunice."

"And the times you got up to drive me to early mass."

"Oh, *noth*ing."

"I remember the dances. Oh, you gave lovely dances, Mrs. Bracken."

"We surely did, yes, we did."

"And your old mother playing the whatsit, the cello, out under the trees."

"You helped me light the paper lanterns, Eunice."

"Yes, it was very pretty. How pretty it was."

"All gone."

"We're not supposed to say anything good about those times but I'd like to say this, Mrs. Bracken: you were always good to me. Mr. Bracken too. He often gave me ten dollars if we had to stay very late. I never let it hurt my feelings."

"You *didn't?*"

"Nor the girls giving me their castoffs and their perfume and stuff they got they didn't like. I never once had hurt pride. Now that we're all gloriously equalized I can tell you this."

"Thank you, Eunice. I'm sure none of us—"

"You've had a wonderful life, Mrs. Bracken."

"Yes, I have."

"You should go happy—"

"I *did* have a wonderful life."

"—remembering your wonderful life and your beautiful apartment in New York with the great huge Persian rugs it used to take hours to vacuum and the silver that took forever to polish and your house here in Bedford and your trips away to Europe—"

"Oh, stop this," Lacey said. "You bitch."

"And your beautiful daughters and a husband who couldn't do enough for you and you shouldn't blame yourself for anything now, even going off with lies and deceit, going off with that man—"

"Oh, get out of here," Lacey screamed and ran out into the hallway and called uselessly up and down the hall to the matron, to someone to get this Irish bitch out of here.

* * *

When Daddy got ill it was very sudden.

One day just not feeling up to par, he said, and so not going down to the office, and the next in a private room in Lenox Hill looking more indignant than ill. Daddy propped up in the half-raised bed looking indignant, his gray-blond hair neatly brushed across his forehead rather like a little boy's and furious at the red tape. "What? You're not leaving, are you?" and when they said visitors' hours, etc., "Ridiculous. Stay on, have a drink or something," Daddy would snort. In between he was flirty with the nurses, especially the abundantly plain night nurse, whom he addressed as "Laraine Day" and said in front of the turnip-faced thing, "See how she takes my pulse? She has a kind of Lana Turner bedside manner."

They knew almost at once there was no hope.

Tess sat beside the bed and felt his death inside her as though she had swallowed a cold raw fish whole. Had she any faith in God, she thought, she would offer anything, anything for his life—stay a virgin forever, tend the lepers in Morotai, anything—and when they were occasionally left alone she wet her lips to say could she get Zina for him? Should she call Zina? She wet her lips to say this thing and beg his forgiveness for her jealousy and for the horrible attitude she had chosen to take to him for the last nine months, since the evening of Mama's recital when he asked her just to understand. In return she had tilted her chin and cast down her eyes with faintly suggested pity (God forgive her) to most everything he said to her; she was just a hair's-breadth from suggesting to him that his adultery had quite possibly scarred her for life. She presented this attitude to him silently like an Arab beggar presenting a sore and now Cordelia-like she wanted to embrace and comfort him, deplore her wicked jealousy and possessiveness—after all, there had never been, would never be a man she would love more. Sometimes he seemed to be waiting for her to speak (and not wait too long, his days slipping away), waiting for her to speak the simple words "I am sorry" and so desperately she wet her lips and brought herself with terrible effort to tell him there was a new elevator operator in the apartment building who aspired to comic heights by announcing floors in the voice of Donald Duck. Every evening she went home with a feeling of despair and rage about herself which she was too young to properly diagnose as the astonishment and resentment at his coming death, of *any* death including her own. It had never occurred to her that she too would die, perhaps stricken suddenly like Daddy, and fade into bones and die. How would she do it? Would anyone be there? Would she know in advance or be knocked down not seeing the truck coming?

Once Daddy opened his eyes and said, "I've been thinking about London all day." Said, "Just as soon's I'm back on my feet let's all go to London and stay at Claridge's and go see the changing of the Guard and go see if the damn ravens are still at the Tower of London and go have roast beef at Simpson's in the Strand."

And, "Roast *beef*," said Mama. "Jack, they still have rationing there and everything is terrible," Mama said. "Why, they are practically starving. Myfanwy Abbott's sister who lives in Hyde Park Lane wrote her the other day she hasn't seen an egg in three months, Jack."

Oh, but pretend we'll go, Tess begged silently, for God's sake pretend to him. He's never needed pretense as much as he needs it now.

"I wouldn't think it was right," Mama said, rearranging some flowers for the worse, "for Americans to go over and take the food from those poor English."

At last Tess took courage at the terrible sight of him, the bones of him fallen against the pillow. She eased into it by saying, "Lacey Edwards is back from Paris." He merely looked weary as if to say don't weigh me down with useless information. She leaned over him and said, "Daddy, do you want Zina to come? Do you want me to call Zina?"

He turned the other way and said in a voice as flat as rain on tin, "Oh, that finished months ago, didn't you guess?"

One evening he woke from a long sleep and turned and groped for her hand and looked at her and said, "Nobody's happy but try to have a good time, will you?"

He died at twenty past seven the next evening while she and Mama were downstairs in the coffee shop, as though not to bother them.

Of course it wasn't true, wasn't true, hadn't happened, she told herself every sickening morning waking up, wasn't him in that (vulgar horrible word) casket and not his clothes Mama packed for the Salvation Army. It was not possible for him not to be in the world, just not possible, she would not accept it, not without a long struggle anyway, and she snubbed the Dalton students who offered her sympathy. Perhaps it was this resolve not to accept it that also undid her because for a while she had no grief, no kindly release of tears, but only a numbness and a feeling that she was wearing something too tight around her forehead. She also had to cope with her mother.

When they came home from the cremation into the huge lonely apartment it seemed at first as if by mutual tacit understanding that they must talk like bare acquaintances.

"I thought Dorothy Dare's red carnations were simply lovely, didn't you, Tiz?"

"Yes, Mama."

"It was good of the Petersons to come all the way down from Albany, especially as she has been so ill all winter. People are terribly thoughtful."

Then they sat in silence for a long while and Mama stared at the Persian rug.

"Ohhhhh." There was a drawn-out note of pain the color of blue, a blue pain. "Ohhhh," Mama said, "he was so kind." She went and stood at the window for a long time with her thin cello-playing hands clasped in front of her. "He was so kind to me you'll never know. When we first met I had just been through something *so*—well, never mind. I often wonder if I did the right thing, that's the point, but—oh, he was so kind. I had been through—well, anyway, I had been very unhappy. I had been through something with a man that —well, anyway, I was, you see, having this affair with someone that—" She shook her head now, seeing him in the cold black glass, seeing this man Tess had never heard of before. "Anyway, I was going to give up going to Leipzig for him. I would have done anything for him, *anything.* And then I heard from someone I barely knew that he was going to be married the next day or the day after or something; this was just in the street from practically a stranger, you see. But I went back home instead of—instead of what I was first going to do and there was Jack, you see, and you see he had been through something similar with some girl and—oh, the kindness of him, the absolute tenderness of Jack Adams was—I want you not to forget Daddy's kindness."

Then it was that Mama walked over to Daddy's marble-topped bar where all the decanters stood with their little silver necklaces. "Daddy's Scotch," she said and poured the first drink of her life and drank it.

And her mother, old Mrs. Van Hoorens, had been a drunk and died of it, so Tess had been told over and over.

When Mama poured a second drink Tess said, "You better be careful, Mama, you're not used to that."

"I am having a little trouble connecting past and present," Mama said. "Maybe this will help.

"He would want me to be helped," Mama said after another long silence, looking at the rug. "Don't you understand that?"

"Yes, Mama."

By dinnertime she was drunk; she took her glass to the table, she had difficulty helping herself to the sliced lamb and vegetables Dora held out, beans and gravy spilled; once her elbow slipped from the table and she very nearly hit her chin on it. Dora's eyebrows were sky high at Tess. Later, when Dora took away Mama's hardly touched dish, Mama said, "You have to forgive me, Dora. I am having trouble con-necting."

"Yes, Mrs. Adams."

Mama smiled sweetly at Dora, smiled sweetly at Tess. "I feel I have been cut off from my past," she said.

Next morning she was so sick and hung over Tess was sure she would never touch liquor again but in the evening she was drunk by dinner and again the following night. "Daddy always wanted me to have a drink, you know," she said. She made rambling non-sequitur phone calls to her friends, startling them with her high-pitched voice. Did I ever tell you what Jack did for me in Paris once? she asked them.

She managed when her friends dropped in to pull herself together; she was with some great effort coherent or at worst mildly tipsy.

"It's the shock," Mama's friends said to Tess in the hall. "It's the grief, poor love."

What about *my* grief? Tess gazed resentfully at them with her wide eyes still unwashed by any tears. What about my ache? I wish *I* could drink. I would drink and drink until I had burned away this solid lump of cold grief which won't move up or down.

"I'm not a psychiatrist," Dr. Ainslee said, "I'm a general practitioner, but you don't need a psychiatrist to diagnose she's just a little distraught over her loss." Dr. Ainslee was as irritable over Tess's alarmed call as if he had been summoned to drive through a blizzard for someone with mild influenza.

"But she doesn't *drink,*" Tess kept saying.

"Seen this kind of thing lots of times," Dr. Ainslee said. "She'll quit when she begins to feel better." He prescribed a mild sedative. But Mama continued to drink. It became a dread to Tess to open the front door when she came home from school.

The only sound in the drawing room before dinner was the big clock and the clink of Mama's glass being put down. Mama was unfailingly gracious.

"Did—you—have a goodtime—last night?"

"I didn't go out last night."

"Oh, I thought you did."

Clink.

"I'll be all right once I can find find my con-connection, dear."

"Mama," Tess said boldly, "if only you'd play something, if only you'd go back to your music."

"No, no." Mama made a gesture of revulsion toward where the cello stood in its case.

"No, no, finished. That's *another* of my regrets. I was always playing cello to him instead of having a *drink* with him, the dear."

"Oh, now, Mama . . ."

"He *wanted* to have a drink with me but no, no. . . ." She played long sweeping chords on an invisible cello. "Ohh, it haunts me. Praps I deserve to be cut off."

"But cut off from what?"

"I don't know, don't ask me. But I'm cut off, I'm adrift, see?"

"*On* a sea, do you mean?"

"*No.*" Mama waved her arms in exasperation. "Don't. Don't." She made pushes in the air, warding Tess off. "Don't *interpret* me that way, mind. I don't wish to be *interpreted.* Please! *You* can't do anything. What can *you* do?"

"I want to try to help you, Mama."

Mama rose quickly, lurched, then crossed to the bar with that

regal hauteur achieved at some states of drunkenness—duchesslike
—slopped whisky into her glass and then flashed the duchess smile
in the general direction of Tess. She was gracious as a perfect
stranger.

"*Terri*fly kind of you, darling."

"Dinner." Dora at the door signaling, eyes to heaven, Jesus.

"Do you know, Dora, splendid as I know it is, dear Dora, I *think*
I'm not the weeniest bit hungry tonight."

"Now, Mrs. Adams—"

"*Per*fectly splendid dinner, I'm sure."

"Mrs. Adams, you gotta *eat* something."

"*Please.*"

"You come to dinner now."

Mama edged away crabwise from Dora and threw her the duchess
look, only scornful. "My husband is the only one who tells me what
to do."

Adrift, rudderless, she lurched from room to room as though she
were looking for him.

Rescue came as is often the case from the least expected quarter.
Lacey Edwards on the phone: "Are we friends or foes?" Tess cool,
hanging onto the last frayed threads of her old resentment of Zina.
"Do you want to see Charles Boyer in *Mayerling* at the Art?" All of
a sudden Tess, squeezed into the guest closet, was gasping it out.
"My mother's drinking, Lacey, she's been drinking for over two
weeks without a stop. I don't know what to do. Oh, I think I'm going
crazy."

"I'll come over."

Then Lacey at the door all in black, too old for her, and wearing
two gold hoop earrings large enough for small birds to swing in.

"She's a bit . . . you know." Tess in the hall. "Pretend you don't
notice."

"Why?"

"Mother, this is Lacey Edwards, a friend of mine."

Mama slewing round startled, the blurred smile.

"Djudo."

"I'm pleased to meet you," Lacey said. "What a lovely apartment."

"Issit? My husband . . . very good taste, you see."

"I knew Mr. Adams," Lacey said boldly and sat down on a footstool near Mama. "He took Tess and me to the museum once."

"Hiddid?" Mama trying to work out Lacey.

"He was one laugh after another," Lacey said ambiguously. "Oh, I love this room. Is this the room you give concerts in, Mrs. Adams?"

"Yes, we used—"

"Uh-huh."

"—to but—"

"But you should have brighter bulbs in here. You ought to have hundred-watt bulbs in a big room like this."

"Perhaps so," Mama said, looking around.

"Pink ones; it makes it more cheerful. A big room like this needs light. Can I have one of these cigarettes? What a cunning box; is it malachite?"

Mama took in Lacey's unrelieved black and said, "Are you in mourning too?"

"Oh, no, I almost always wear black. Could I have some tea, do you suppose?"

Lacey gave this to Tess as a cue to leave.

"Could we have it in a pot, do you suppose?"

By the time Tess came back with the tea, Lacey was saying, "If I was to tell you who my father is you'd fall right off that chair." When Mama reached for her empty glass, Lacey got brazenly up and took it away from her. "Oh, no, you said you were going to have *tea* with me, Mrs. Adams. Oh, please do." Lacey handed Mama tea and gave the glass to Tess with another jerk of her earrings toward the door.

"I'll see if we have any cookies," Tess said and stayed away a long time. When she brought the cookies Lacey was saying, "It's all a matter of finding out how you manage all by yourself in a situation like mine. My mother and I are on completely different wavelengths." Mama, sipping tea, was taking Lacey in more easily.

66

Lacey had turned the tables. "My whole life has been just self-survival, Mrs. Adams," she said. "Do you mind me telling you all this?" and Mama said no, of course not. Mama was all ears. She was staring down at Lacey, sitting at her feet, and her thin breast was rising and falling quickly with the intakes of her breaths of emotion. For she was being appealed to, perhaps for help, for understanding, and it had never happened before. Mama was always the protected one. Her family had fussed over and protected her because of her precious talent and then Daddy had protected her all their married life and even Tess had protected her by not confiding anything to her. It was as though she had been an invalid lying in a silent room while everyone tiptoed around so as not to disturb her and now Lacey was asking for her understanding and this had reached a secret unlit place in Mama's heart and illuminated it with perhaps a lovely and also terrifying communication.

Mama said, "Child," most tenderly to Lacey; she obviously was shaken to the depths by this appeal to her. She had temporarily forgotten death and herself.

As Tess left the room, Lacey got up and closed the door; so then, sitting in the hall, Tess could only hear continuing murmurs.

Then, a long time later, the low sweet sounds of a cello.

"Tess!"
"Can I come in a minute?"
Now Zina Edwards was looking at *her* in the same astounded way Mama had been looking at Lacey.

"Lacey's not home," Zina said.

"There's something I want to say to *you*," Tess said. She had decided in a moment, flung on a coat and run. Something had to be put right between her and Zina for Daddy's sake. So, standing rigid as though she had on a mortarboard and were about to make her commencement speech, she heard herself saying, "My father would have wanted . . ." her voice sounding dubbed, fakey, thick, as if her mouth were full of peanut butter, using phrases like "whereas to the contrary"; overelegant, stiff apologies for her behavior spoken into a cathedral of silence because, of course, Zina was appalled at the priggishness of it, the spectacle she was making of herself with this oratory which both of them knew was specious bunkum because she had no more come to apologize than she had come to make friends with Zina. She thoroughly disliked Zina and had made it abundantly clear and so to stand here in Zina's drawing room and mouth pious apologies was adding insult to injury in the most uncivil way and to drag in the dead body of her father and lay it between them on the carpet was desecration, to impose herself and her tiny aggrievements on what had been a greater love, a greater tragedy, was to impugn that love. To stand in this room where there had been vibrations of love and passion and hurt enough to crack the ceiling and call attention to her own hurt was the equivalent of showing to someone with a terminal illness one's tennis knee. And Daddy would have been furious beyond words, he would have taken hold of her and shaken her, probably.

And every time she referred to him, my father this, my father that, the stranger he sounded to her; the more she claimed him the more foreign he became, receding into the far distance, and became a slight acquaintance, blurry (and on this yellow sofa he must have laid his head on Zina's breast, right here on these yellow pillows he must have told her all sorts of secret things), and all the time Zina listened silently and more and more it became apparent they had not known the same John Adams and Zina suffering her in politeness and she really would have liked to smash her fist in Zina's pointed face and once and for all tell her how much she hated her, despised her for knowing her father better than she, but little black dots had begun jumping around on Zina's face and the walls had begun dancing a bit and then hot water started streaming from her eyes and next thing she knew she was on her knees, bag falling open, drowning in this cascade and finding her head in Zina's lap and hearing these braying sounds she was making and then long gulping sobs, the kind that broken-hearted children cry in spurts and hiccups, hardly able to draw breath between the bone-racking spasms of ecstatic grief.

Zina said, "Now I think a bit of sherry wouldn't do any harm."

Zina was very patient with her. When she appeared to be on the verge of another paroxysm, Zina said sip your sherry or pointed suddenly across the room and said go over and look at that little picture, it's by a friend of mine, do you like it? She took off her shoes and had a second sherry, sitting on the sofa, and they had an interesting talk about love. It was almost unnerving to find herself on the brink of liking Zina and Zina telling her in a cool unemotional way what she thought about people's needs for love, about so much of it being a myth really and honestly; so much of it only because it is unthinkable *not* to love. Just occasionally Zina would say your father didn't understand this or that. Then she would leave off and walk over to a plant and snap off a leaf and say it wasn't doing very well, this or that plant. One had to admit her attractions, her grace and detachment. Well, we all need something, she said, and gathered the multicolored chiffon folds around her, we all have to feel connected to something and if it isn't love then something else, the way, she supposed, some people become nuns or else the way some people have to make do with making enormous money or achieving power over other people. "Sometimes I think they feel forced to feel they have missed something," Zina said. "I knew a most powerful statesman once who cried in his sleep.

"In other words," Zina said as Tess leaned, soothed, on the marble hall stand, dawdling, delaying going, "what I'm saying is that a huge lot of nonsense is written about love and talked about love and God knows sung about love and we are all indoctrinated with it. I wonder why civilization isn't sick to the living death of it."

Did you bring an umbrella? No? Well, listen, come again anytime, Zina said, bending into nasturtiums at the door, and then straightened up and put orange nasturtiums into her hand and said as if she were suddenly angry over all this waste of time, all this hand-wringing over love, "What's important is compassion," she said. "Nobody *really* cries for anyone else, don't believe it, not even you for your father. We cry for ourselves. Cold tears for ourselves. If you can really cry for someone else, my God, you might start to be happy."

"Your mother," Tess told Lacey on the phone (because she had been thinking about it and it was a revelation to her), "told me the most marvelous thing. She said I don't really have any compassion and when I learn how I can cry for someone else, *really*, really cry for someone else, I might *begin* to be happy."

"Oh, she's always coming out with some great *wisdom*," Lacey said.

*　*　*

So now time was up.

"Time is up, girls," the matron said, squishing into the visitors' room at Biding, where Tess and Lacey had only really begun to get talking, and the Ladiesaid girl put away her crocheting.

"We have to go now, dear," the Hooper girl said.

"Well," Tess said.

"Well," Lacey said.

They stood up and they laced fingers and walked behind the big-bottomed matron and the Ladiesaid guard to as far as where a sign said RESIDENTS NOT ALLOWED BEYOND THIS GATE.

Here they hugged. But it was better not to say anything and anyway, what was there to say? Good-bye? So long? Happy to have known you? Lacey's mouth was working as though she were rinsing out with a very tart mouthwash and Tess thought it was emotion until Lacey leaned to kiss her and hissed in her ear, "Tess, as you won't be needing them, could I have the rest of your real cigarettes?"

The Katonah Country Club was on the eighteenth floor of the new IT&T building on what had once been Mount Holly Road. Tess and Hooper were sucked into the air-bubble elevator along with the very influential. Only the very influential could belong to the Katonah Country Club. Only the Harry Platts and the great could afford not only the dues but the danger of their being thought to be reactionar-

70

ies. The Katonah Country Club was a reproduction. A bright fire crackled in a fireplace exactly like the real thing; there was a long oak bar, oaken beams and windows that looked out on rolling green lawns and a golf course, trees and ponds. Only of course the space outside the windows was barely a foot deep and the effect was created stereoscopically along with recordings of birds and faint cries of "Fore" and if you pressed a button a doll's rainstorm beat against the glass. For astronomical prices you could get real honest-to-God food, not badly cooked.

The smiling hostess in a long dress came forward, baring her teeth.

"Mrs. Bracken, is it? Come this way, dear. Mr. Platt has a table by the window. What a lovely day for you, dear."

As they passed through, Tess saw another old person being given the farewell luncheon. He was weakly refusing cake and weeping while the relatives cajoled him.

Harry Platt stood up politely.

"Ah, Tessa. Here you are."

It might have been a Sunday luncheon long ago. Flowers on the table. Big menus were brought. Green turtle soup, she read. Rack of lamb Provençal. Curry of shrimp.

Barbara said, "Let Mother sit facing the view."

They had tranquilized Joan, who sat blinking dully.

Harry held Tess's chair politely while she sat down.

On the plate was the form letter from the White House. "Dear Mrs. Brackin [spelled wrong] : Today, like Columbus, you start on a journey of tremendous importance and—"

She put it down unread.

Now, Harry said, she must have whatever she liked, implying nothing was too good, too expensive. First, would she care for the herring from Alaska? It was good.

It was not the only good thing about Alaska, she wanted to say grimly. Alaska, still being underpopulated, had no laws about forced euthanasia as yet.

"What is this place?" Joan asked thickly. "Where are we?"

71

It is hell, she wanted to say.

It wasn't so much the gourmet lunch, the forced feeding, the gesture that made the gorge rise but the total lack of shame they had about it, the gross unfeeling, the impertinence of their thinking they were being gracious. It was the terrifying sincerity of their believing they were kindly and expensively putting themselves out for you.

She felt she had to make one gesture of reproach.

With enormous disdain, she threw her menu on the floor. There was a second or two of frightened silence at the table and then Harry bent to pick up the menu, unruffled, smiled at her and put his arm gently around her shoulders while with his other hand he undid her clenched fingers and fitted the menu into it. "Now I'll tell you what we'll have first," Harry said. *"First* we'll have good behavior."

* * *

When Harry Platt followed Elton into the room, they at first didn't recognize him. There was nothing at a quick glance to identify the eager ice cube vendor with this carefully Brooks-Brothers-dressed young man (except the tie, Tess thought, the tie was not up to the expectations of the suit and by their ties ye shall know them) with his hair slightly longer and not slicked down; better-looking and strangely taller, Tess thought, and then noticed he was wearing shoes with lifts, which served to emphasize his manikin walk. He shook hands with them formally. His manner was as quietly changed for the better as his clothes; his manner was gray-flanneled and assured. Merry Christmas, he said and Tess thought there was a glimmer of restitution-at-last in the way he said it.

"He thought he mightn't be welcome," Elton said.

It was over a year since Harry Platt had dropped out of their lives. He'd come up to Elton on the train, asked after Tess and the girls, thought he mightn't be welcome. Nonsense, Elton said. Where did he get that idea? Besides, it was Christmas Eve. Anyway, there was no taxi at the station. Sit down, sit down, Elton said and sent Barbara to get Harry eggnog. Harry Platt sat down and crossed his legs carefully so as not to spoil the crease in his pants; perhaps also to let them see his expensive Sulka hosiery with clocks. He had the grace of somebody who has made something of himself. He *had* made something of himself. What had he been up to? He had to pause for effect. Well, he was with B and K. B and K? Advertising, Harry said. Not a big outfit, not J. Walter Thompson, but nevertheless some nice accounts, and he was getting experience. Maybe they had seen the commerical in which a tiny child shampooed a huge Saint Bernard into a mountain of lather with a thimbleful of liquid? That was Harry's creation. But why would one delegate a tiny child to shampoo a Saint Bernard? Joan asked him, looking down at him from the ladder by the Christmas tree. Isn't that a mite whimsical of you? she asked, but Harry had grown careful and didn't answer. He took a sip of eggnog and then put it down with the infinitesimal implication that it was too sweet and when Tess dropped a log she was carrying to the fire he made no move to help her pick it up.

"Well, Harry," Joan said, "you've made quite a metamorphosis, haven't you? I think we'll call you Harry the Met," Joan said and took a tinsel star and crowned Harry with it but Harry only smiled tolerantly and when the other people started coming, Andrew la Farge and the Kelly girls and other people he had known in the days when he was snubbed by them and made himself a laughingstock, he responded coolly, shaking hands and saying Hi, Hello, How're *you?* He was cold. He let them know he was their equal.

Exactly at the right time, it seemed, he knew when to withdraw; asked if he might call a taxi.

Of course, Tess said, relieved.

But he didn't remember exactly where the phone was in the hall, he said. So come, Tess said, and I'll show you and took him into the hall and picked up the phone for him. Call 7770, she said and thanks, Harry said and walked right past her and into the hall toilet and she realized he had left her to do it; he had scored and she found herself saying could they send a cab to the Bracken house. Not a big thing but coolly planned and a trap is a trap no matter how shallow. Well, it had only been a chance meeting on the train, she told herself, and he was ensconced in New York, so there was little to fear about him trying once more to attach himself to them. And what did it matter anyway? He was simply a dull young man. No, not dull; opaque. Opaque and ambitious and cold and after some prize.

And the prize was in their house, Tess told herself, unable to deny that she felt cold. In the pantry taking down stirrup cups, her hands were all fingers and thumbs and she smashed one of the cups in the sink, thinking about Harry Platt and having one of those spooky tics that foretold the future.

Harry was not finished with them by a long shot.

"Don't encourage him to come again, Barbara," she said and Barbara said in her sharp way (intensely involved in Women's Lib, she read chauvinism into everything) do you think I'm man hunting? "Why would *I* want to encourage him?" Barbara asked and gave a shudder as though a tarantula had walked between her breasts. Nevertheless after Harry's visit, if you were quick, she could be caught staring into fires, into space, with the look of someone who has got all dressed up and then not been called for.

"Where, oh, where, is Harry the Met? On a cold and frosty morning," Joan sang.

But Harry didn't come.

To Tess's relief he made no appearances over the holidays nor the whole of January and when February went by she felt these spooky hunches of hers had been false alarms. She didn't believe in fate or *deus ex machina*. It became obvious Harry Platt had dropped them for bigger game.

Then Harry's voice said America's rotten. "I think we're on the verge of a huge moral crisis," Harry's voice said outside on the veranda and Tess spilled the drink she had been carrying to Elton. "I agree," her husband said.

She stood absolutely rigid with disappointment and the feeling of heaviness Harry gave one.

"Not just in the political sense," Harry said, "but deep in our fiber. Do you get the feeling that something out of all proportion is going to happen?"

She stood in her pink-lit safe living room, fire crackling and

"Sesame Street" playing to itself on the TV, and heard Harry saying a lot about God and country and love of the President and the pinko bias of the Eastern press and TV people who were organized to attack every fundamental American principle and were using *humor* to do it, which was pretty dirty pool, Harry said. It was Harry's opinion that the State Department was thick as fleas with homosexuals. "I'd burn out those queers first thing of all," Harry said. He made a token gesture of rising when Tess came out the door and handed Elton his drink. "Hello, Harry," she said and didn't offer him the usual ginger ale. "You'll stay and have a bite with us, won't you?" Elton asked and Harry said why, yes, if he wasn't being *de trop*. He was wearing (she noticed when they sat down to the soup) a Norfolk jacket of expensive woven fabric but had had his nails manicured and colorless varnish applied to them and if she had had a sop of tenderness toward him she would perhaps have told him this was a stamp of the very bourgeois thing he was trying to escape. Otherwise his manners were impeccable although he paid only the minimum attention required to her and Barbara. There was something innately nineteenth century in his manner toward women and Barbara had to have sensed it; her face was red and she crumbled bread continuously as Harry directed all his talk to Elton. His questions were diligent and searching and when he gave an opinion it was, he gracefully implied, only to be regarded in proportion to his own lack of experience, but several times Elton said why, I think that's using your noodle, Harry, or by God, I feel the same way. Harry seemed to have either done extensive research on Elton or was possessed of catlike intuition; time and again he expressed Elton's opinions (phrased as queries: Elton's own thoughts being posed to him as questions). By God, Elton said, I'm going to speak to Gittelson about you at McRand; we are lawyers for them. By gum, Tess, I think they ought to find a place for Harry, don't you?

"Pass the mint sauce, would you?" she said, furious with Elton.

"You certainly let him maneuver you into that," she said after Harry left.

"Now, Tess," Elton said, "here's a young feller starts out selling ice cubes and gets to be an executive producer for an advertising firm as fast as that, why, that's Horatio Alger, dearest, that's the American way."

You could not explain intangibles to him; dear and all as he was, the intangible was wasted on Elton Bracken. There was no way to express her panic.

"I like his ideas," Elton said.

So Harry moved up to McRand. His note of thanks was a triumph of courteous salutation. It could have been cast in bronze and inserted under a statue of Elton.

"I don't see what you've got against him," Elton said.

In the spring he started coming again on Sundays and ran around the tennis court in his peculiar diving dogged run, smashing and lobbing without enjoyment as if the balls were grenades.

"Oh, I can't get *over* him," Joan said. She still treated him with a kind of amused contempt but she no longer tried to put him down.

"Oh, it's really rather sweet," she said when someone said wasn't his Toyota a bit *too* red.

"He's going through a red *phase*," Joan said. She watched him with little gurglings of amusement; almost protective, she threw in an occasional vindication of him: "Harry's got nice legs when he's walking away from you." "Harry's got not an uncute little ass, have you noticed?"

Once after a protracted silence in the thick late heat of the afternoon, when everyone had pretty much decided no more tennis, she sprang up suddenly, seized her racket and hit Harry on the knee with it and said loudly, "Come on and play me to the death and let's see which one of us can kill the other."

And it had been exactly that, with Joan and Harry out for each other's blood, and Joan when she bothered was a first-class tennis player. But Harry responded equally to her challenge, flatfooted and all. It was as if some epic consideration were weighing the outcome as the two figures darted and smashed at each other with a ferocious intensity made even more eerie by the fact that halfway through, the sky darkened with a coming storm and lightning flickered over the two battlers. Twice Joan hit Harry square on, twice he sent her reeling back with a savagely unexpected smash return, and in be-

tween the little green tongues of summer lightning the crash of ball
on gut began to sound like rifle shots. It may have been the failing
light that made some people think Joan threw Harry the game. In
any event, Harry won by the narrow margin she allowed him; he was
limping and panting. Joan threw her racket into a hydrangea bush.
As far as can be remembered, she never played again in her life.

There was something quite unpleasant about the match.

At dinner, Tess, turning her head, caught sight of Joan watching
Harry. The candle burning down low into red glass was on a level
with his face, suffusing it where he sat beside her, his elbow on the
table and his chin cupped in his hand, his gaze directed away from
Joan toward the dark garden. Joan had pushed back her chair from
the table and was lolling back in it so that she was slightly behind
him, one arm limp on the arm of the chair, the other limp on the
table. She seemed half asleep, drowsing, languorously turning the
stem of her wine glass round and around, and all the time she gazed
directly at the back of Harry's neck around the ear, where the skin
was smooth and in the red candlelight an apricot color and silky as
a baby's, taut where the cartilage was, and where the hair, burned
fair by the sun, grew in softish whorls, golden at the ends and darker
underneath where it veed into his collar in a clean line. Joan's mouth
was slightly open and the tip of her tongue ran around her top lip,
exploring, while all the time her half-closed eyes gazed at Harry's
neck as if she would in a minute run a finger under where the hair
curled, and in the flickering red her face seemed shriveled with the
intensity, the look of such sexuality as Tess had scarcely ever seen
in her life.

"Are you both home? Is Father there?"

"Yes, yes. Where are you?"

"Well, you better get him on too."

She put down the phone, knowing. She went out and called downstairs.

"Elton, pick up, will you?"

"What?"

"Pick up the phone. It's Joan."

"Hello?"

"Daddy?"

"Hello, pet. Where are you?"

"I dunno exactly; somewhere in Maryland, I think. Are you on, Mother?"

"Yes."

"Well, then—we're married."

"Maryland, pet? What the hell are you doing in Maryland?"

"Yes, I knew it the minute—"

"What?"

"I just said we're married."

"Married?"

"Shh, Elton. I said I knew. I don't know, it just—the minute you—"

"Married, darling?"

"Yes, Daddy."

"Andy, is it?"

"Oh, Elton, don't be—"

"Harry."

"Which?"

"I'll let you speak to him in a minute. Darling, I'm happy in the wildest way; we both think it's the wildest thing we've ever done in our lives, don't we? I'm telling him it's wild—"

"Which Harry?"

"Which Harry! Oh, Daddy, come *on."*

"Elton, Harry Platt—your protégé."

"Harry *Platt?"*

"Yes, Daddy. I'll let you speak to him in a minute. We decided over lunch and—hello?"

"Yes."

"We're here."

"It's—I'm sorry about the shock and all but, oh—I'm completely —just a minute, say hello to him—they want to say hello to you."

"Hello, Mother. Hello, Father."

"Hello, Harry."

"Hello, Harry."

"Well, my God, this is pretty much of a jump, isn't it?"

"Sir?"

"I said this is a bit of a jump, Harry. I mean—I'm not out of date, I hope, but I would have thought in *your* case you might have had a word with me."

"Yes, I realize that, sir."

"I mean—"

"Daddy—I'm on the other extension—it isn't Harry's fault. We just *decided*—"

"Why exactly in *my* case, sir?"

"What?"

"Just a minute, Joan, I'm asking Father why me?"

"Anybody, Harry. I realize Joan is over eighteen and all that but I just think even in this day and age the decent thing is to come to me and damn well say look here, I want to marry your—"

"Oh, sweetheart, you are funny, Daddy. Mother, are you still on?"

"Yes."

"Well, why aren't you saying anything?"

"Ahem, I don't—can't really think of anything to say."

"Aren't you pleased?"

"Well—"

"I want to speak to Mother a minute alone. Kiss, kiss, kiss."

"What?"

"For you, Daddy. Kiss, kiss, kiss."

"Oh. Kiss, kiss, my sweetheart. I love you, darling girl."

"I know you do, my sweetheart Daddy."

"Kiss, kiss, my girl, even though you ought to have a good spanking. Where the hell are you going to live? What the hell are you going to live on?"

"Kiss, kiss. Now get off. I want to speak to Mother a minute alone, girl talk. Harry?"

"Yes."

"Get off the extension so you won't get any sweller-headed."

"Kiss, kiss, angel, naughty girl, running off like something—old

79

movie or play—ridiculous when we could've given you the big country club slam-bang—"

"Elton, she wants to speak to me alone a minute."

"Yes."

"Are you alone, Mother? Is he off the—"

"Yes, I think so."

"Mother, this is a *man* I have married. Mother?"

"Yes."

"I think you know what I mean. I know you don't like him but he is a man in every sense of the word, thrilling and everything I have ever in my life dreamed of having, period."

"I see."

"Oh, Mother, don't be so lukewarm. He is *nice* too."

"I'm glad."

"Mother—"

"Joan, you know I can't be untruthful, you know that, don't you?"

"Yes, that's why I wanted to tell you alone that you are wrong about him; he is the warmest, the most—for one thing, *entre nous,* the strictly most fabulous thing in bed I have ever—"

"Joan."

"What?"

"I'm upset, darling, I'm going to hang up now. It'll take a little while to get used to it, that's all. Joan, I have to say the truth. Darling, I'm sorry but I'm not happy about it. I'm sorry, Joanie, but I can't say a lie. I'm not happy about it. I'm—"

"Lacey?"

"Yes. Oh, Tess, is it?"

"Did I wake you up?"

"No, I'm watching *For Whom the Bell Tolls* on Channel Nine."

"Joan got married today. To Harry Platt."

"No!"

"Huhh."

"Tess, are you joshing?"

"No. In Maryland somewhere or other they don't make them wait for—"

"Oh, God."

"Yes."

"Had you any inkling?"

"Not exactly."

"Idiot girl. Of course, they're *all* mindless, crazy, this generation. What does Elton think?"

"Oh, upset about—have to keep my voice down—cross about the unimportant end of it, protocol—them not telling us first—but he's somewhat of a champion of Harry, you know."

"A good deal Elton's fault. Tell him I said so."

"Can't see the woods for—he thinks Harry will be very bigwig one of these days."

"Yes, but oh, Christ, having him in the family. Oh, God, I'm sorry for you but oh, *God,* I'm glad I don't have children; I could get on my knees that I didn't get married and have the brats everyone has today."

Barbara said, licking her lips, following Tess into the kitchen, "Well, she's only made herself into a chattel, that's all." Barbara began laughing. Her eyes seemed as bright as if she had put belladonna in them. Her hands twitched as she slammed bread in the toaster.

"Even the ceremony is a *farce.* It's an outrage to the female sex. Not that *I* care about who Joan marries—she could marry the Pope, for all I care—but it is the ceremony that is *obscene.* 'I now pronounce you man and *wife.'* So it's a role. Not *husband* and wife. *Man* and wife. Not even the decency of man and *woman.*"

Up popped the toast angrily. Barbara flashed a knife over it, gnashed into it. So loud were Barbara's teeth tearing into dry toast, chomping on it, that the rest of her words were not clear; something about Harry Platt the pig and so fuggim, Barbara said, tearing into toast as if it were Harry Platt's flesh.

It came on little cat feet; it just came about. Nothing happened like the Reichstag fire. Some people said it was the natural outcome of a democratic republic trying to be empirical; more likely, others

said, it was the natural outcome of an empire trying to be a democratic republic. But out of the chaos came Senator Bjelke-Petersen
of Minnesota, who had a strong cleft chin and a very strong appeal
for the rotarybluehairkiwanistuesdaynightbowling antirevolutionists
and who said that while he deplored the Latin American wars, nevertheless our strength lay in supporting *right*. None of it was new
enough to cause more than mild concern and when Tess said it
frightened her a little, these rallies shown on television where
thousands of mild kitchen-apron grannies and potbellied boys
mingling with drum majorettes jumped up and down waving pla-
cards in one astrodome after another, Elton said oh, but, darling,
there's nothing new about it, said there are people who are desperate to believe, to follow *something;* why, you could get this
crowd to protest frankfurters and support the baked bean if you
had enough gift of oratory and at *least* Petersen is doing something to try to get us out of this mess. And Elton voted for him
because he had no use for the slightly shifty-eyed Senator Kid-
der. After Bjelke-Petersen was hugely elected, it looked as if
normalcy was coming about, fields were getting greener and fair
winds taking the ship of state into safe harbors (what was one to
make of a President who used all three metaphors in the space of
one short paragraph? anyway, about a President who said, about
the Constitution, that it was a pretty swell document, all things
considered, but just the same you had to remember that *any*thing
over two hundred years old just *could* be a little old hat) and it
wasn't for a while that the White House statements began to be
of the type to make some people not believe their ears. It wasn't
thought to be truly serious that actual consideration was being
given to a bill to enact small amendments to the First Amend-
ment. People were vague on television about exactly what was
being done to them. "Can you tell me what is the First Amend-
ment?" the newscaster asked the pretty stenographer, wind blowing her hair this way and that across her face. "The First Amend-
ment is—um—Thou shalt have no other gods before me."

First these things happen in imagination, then on television, then on the streets outside and finally in your own home; it is finally happening to us right in our own home, she thought. They sat in the library, she and Elton, not saying a word, just listening to the voices going on behind the closed doors to the living room. Once Matty came to the door and said, "Would you like me to serve dinner?" "No," Tess said. "We'll have to hold dinner back a while." Matty sighed and went out. From behind the doors they heard Barbara yelling invective.

In between, Harry's voice went on in a monotone, like someone delivering a long prepared speech, then Barbara erupting again and sometimes words were spat through the door: "fascist" and "filthy." "Do your worst," Barbara yelled once. "Oh, go on and do your worst."

Joan came in during one of Barbara's outbursts, stopped in the door and put a hand to her head.

"Still going on?"

"Still going on."

"Oh, why does she antagonize him? It'll only make things worse for her. Listen, I've learned: don't antagonize him. Get *around* him."

"She's fighting for her life," Tess said, astonished that that was it, in a nutshell.

"Well, so have I been," Joan said and picked up the whiskey decanter. "For eight years now, and there's a better way to do it than antagonize him, *believe* me."

"Do you want some water with that?"

"No, thanks."

Joan gazed out the window, Elton flipped the evening paper from time to time, Tess frowned at her fingernails.

"Your petunias have done well this year, Mother."

"Uhum. I've got a new man comes now. Doby was never very good with the petunias."

"So go to hell, go to hell and back," Barbara shrilled.

"I mean"—Elton raised thin hands from the paper into the air—

"what is so terrible about her being on this *list?*"

"It's a list contrary to—" Tess began.

"I wish *I* were on a list," Joan said. "I wish I were on a list of people going to the moon."

"I'm going in," Elton said.

"No, don't."

Elton got up and opened the door and said, "I think this ought to stop now and incidentally this is my house and we are all being kept waiting for dinner."

Harry gave one of his sweetest smiles. "Just—just a little longer, Father. We're almost through."

"*You're* almost through, you mean," Barbara said. She was squatting on the floor in her Honduras khakis and her eyes seemed to be whirling like long-ago Bugs Bunny after hitting a wall. "You and your Petersens and your microfilm inputs on—"

Harry closed the door.

Matty appeared in the hallway. "Mrs. Platt, the little boy's crying."

"Oh, God," Joan said and put down her glass. "All right, I'll come."

"What should we do?" Elton asked. "I mean, do we just sit and let—"

"I *think*," Tess said, having no plan, things having at last come to this, in their own house, as if the blackshirts had marched in, "perhaps dinner."

"No; I want to know what he's saying to her, I want to know what is going on," Elton said. "I can't eat dinner when I don't know the outcome of something, you know that. What's this about Sea Island? That's in Georgia, isn't it? What did he mean about Sea Island?"

"I don't know."

"What the hell goes on in Sea Island?"

"I don't *know*, Elton."

The door flew open. Harry stumped out with his peculiar right arm/leg, left arm/leg march. "Going to be O.K.," he said. He gave them a cheerful wink. The wink was worse, made Tess go cold. He marched out into the hall and picked up the phone.

"I won't go," Barbara said, coming into the room. "I won't."

"Darling, go where?"

"What?"

"Sea Island."

"What in God's name for? Why should you?"

"I am not having a mental breakdown, Father."

"Babsy, of course you are not. Who says you are?"

But she was very jerky, they noticed. One shoulder twitched up suddenly to her neck. Barbara had jerked herself into a chair, where she sat twisted around as if she had suffered a mild stroke. One arm twitched now, her knee jerked. "I am not ill."

"Get her a drink, Elton."

"I don't want a drink. I am not going to that place. You know what they do to them there."

"Here, darling. Calm down now, Barby. What place? Where? I don't know what anybody is talking about."

"Physiotherapy."

"What for?"

"Who is he calling?"

Barbara jerked up and twisted into the hall. "Who are you calling?"

Tess and Elton followed and all three stood around Harry, talking on the phone.

"Look *here*—" Elton said but Harry merely held up a finger to admonish him. Nobody knew who or why Harry was phoning.

Dimly, Matty made a motion to Tess from the distant pantry. "No," Tess called out. "You'll have to keep dinner back. I don't *know* when."

Harry hung up the phone and said, "Going to be easier than you think, Barbs."

"I won't go," Barbara said and ran into the living room. "It's a kind of psychic lobotomy."

"Now do you think for a *minute*—" Harry was saying gently, lifting his hands to his head to ward off their threats and their frightened protests. "Quiet, quiet—do you mind, Dad, do you mind, Mother?"

"There's *no way,*" Barbara said, shaking her head from side to side.

"—think that I would make her go anyplace I didn't *know* was perfectly *guaranteed* under FHL? It's a rest place in one of the loveliest hotels on one of the old Sea Island estates. Now, Mother Bracken, *you* know Mrs. Morris Underwood; isn't she an old buddy of yours?"

"I haven't seen her in a long—"

"Do you think *she* would go anyplace they do things that are not according to Hoyle?"

"If she doesn't want to go—" Elton began.

"Salt baths," Harry said sweetly. "Hot salt baths, rest and exercise with qualified nurses—"

They said all the expected things: they were her parents, they certainly had some say in the matter, they would refuse permission, they would call the police, lay charges against Harry. They were like two minor characters in a Donizetti opera, waving their hands and speaking in unison, often incoherently. Then two hefty women in white were actually standing in the doorway and Barbara had stood up and given a peculiar smile, still shaking her head from side to side but with this gingerly smile little children sometimes use to those they distrust, and then flew toward the door to the garden, but already one of the muscular dames was there before her and Barbara dodged and ran the other way toward the library door, but the other woman darted to bar the way and now the two of them advanced slowly on her and Barbara, still smiling and cornered, stepped behind the encyclopedia stand as Elton got hold of one of the white-coated ladies by the back of her belt but then Harry, shorter by half a head than Elton but stocky strong, had embraced Elton from behind and they had gone into a sort of dance until Harry, holding Elton by the shoulders, was pinning him to the mantel and they had knocked over the encyclopedia stand and Barbara was being walked toward the front door in a jumpy rubber-legged way and all the time

Tess hung onto her by the jacket with one hand and tried to push at the nurses with the other and found herself being jerked along with the whole parcel of them until in the hallway one of the Indian rugs ruckled up under her and she fell on her face.

*   *   *

A hum had settled over the dining room of the Katonah Country Club; it was the hum of modulated voices talking boneless, opinionless conversation.

"I think I'm going to have the seafood pie," Barbara said. She wore a continuous smile. "What are *you* going to have, Harry? Mother? Joan? This is nice, isn't it? Isn't this pleasant? I love this room. When were we here last? Was it Joan's birthday? Anyway, I can remember everything I had. I had the spinach soup and the seafood pie and a *real* banana for dessert and we had the nonalcoholic sangría. Oh, yum yum yum, everything looks so good. Have you been here before, Hooper? Isn't it nice, the way they've done it? It's an exact copy of the real place. My father wouldn't know any different, would he, Mother? He wouldn't notice a speck of difference. Oh, I love these plastic dishes, they're so silent, and look, they're willow pattern, isn't that cunning? What are you going to have, Joan?"

Barbara was tying a paper bib around Joan's neck and Joan looked at her groggily.

"Can I have a drink?" Joan asked.

"Were you going to say something, Harry?"

"No, Barb. When everyone's decided, I'd like to say grace."

"Oh, sorry sorry. Quick quick. Oh, yum yum yum, what'll I have first?"

"I'll have a double gall and wormwood on the rocks," Joan said. Tess stared at the menu.

I wish I could *feel* something, she thought. Beyond the fear; the

87

fear is such a dull thing. I wish I could feel something about *them,* about Harry even. It would be *bigger* if I could feel something about Harry beyond hate. Something bigger than that. It would help to put things together before I go. I would love to put things together. Like my two broken children. In some way *I'm* something to do with it, something I didn't do. I only loved them. What I think I mean is I *only* loved them and if I could clearly put it together I think that that was not enough. I served them love, like dinner. I didn't work at it. I didn't really *look* at them to see what was there. Just *loving.* Not much different than just voting. What could *I* do about Joan? What could *I* do about the President? Nothing. We *all* did nothing. Is that what's brought us to this pass? No. But there's a link somewhere. Something about children standing apart and you don't interfere with them, just love them. Love them, feed them, educate them, let them go; that's all you're expected to do, isn't it? That's what everybody did. But somehow there's something wrong with it. We all just stood around and said nice things to each other and remembered birthdays and sent Christmas cards and had quarrels and made up and behaved decently and felt that this is all it *is.* But it isn't. And there's a link, a link. Just the same as all the families make all the nations make the world. Not enough. Just as it's not enough to blame the men for what happened because they were too busy watching the Mets play Chicago. Just as it's not enough just to hate Harry. There must be something much more important than just hating Harry and if I could find it . . .

No answer.

Only the waiter bending over her and saying, "I can recommend the *ham.*" And a little clap of pretend thunder outside the "window" and rain. She jumped. He had said it with such a strange innuendo: "the *ham.*" He had a glass eye and it took her about five beats of the heart to place him. She couldn't remember his name but they'd called him Cyclops, hadn't they? Ham's friend from—

"Why, it's—" she began but he quickly put a finger to his lips. *Ham.*

"Imported from *Canada,*" the waiter said. Well, Ham *was* from

Canada. He was trying to tell her something but the others were watching so he took the orders.

"Anything," she said.

Steamed codfish was ordered for her.

Then while Harry was saying a long grace and heads were bent, the waiter scribbled something on a card and slipped it under her water glass and taking a sip of water she picked it up and held it in her lap and tried to read it but without her glasses it was a blur. What an odd thing. But then if it really *was* Ham, it wasn't odd at all. Even if this had only been at Schrafft's and not in these alarming times, this would have been like Ham. Ham had had her paged at her wedding.

She managed to get down a few mouthfuls of the codfish and then (her heart was beating so, she felt it could be heard) she asked to be excused to go to the ladies' room.

When she got there, accompanied, of course, by the ever-present Hooper, she went into a toilet and shot the bolt (for years now the only true privacy had been the john, the only place you could be alone, and even then you had to be careful it wasn't TV-monitored) and putting on her glasses read *Ham St Thomas Mt Kisco 5.*

Sat down and read it over and over.

"Don't be *too* long, pet," Hooper said outside the door.

If it meant—

But surely Ham couldn't be still alive. He was older than she, at least five years. She had told herself years ago, hearing nothing in ages (although that was not unlike him), that Ham must be dead, "called for" years ago. But then Ham was *Canadian.*

Five o'clock, did it mean? Mount Kisco? Was there still a Saint Thomas's Church in Mount Kisco?

"Come on, dear, please don't get me into trouble, now," Hooper said through the door in a whining tone. "Be a good girl, sweetheart."

Oh, my God, she thought, of *all* people to try to come to my rescue. Ham, who always tricked me. A bag of tricks, always.

She began to shake with laughter. Covering her mouth, she leaned against the cold wall of the toilet and laughed and laughed, and it may have sounded like illness because Hooper said, "Are you sick, dear?"

"Yes," she said. "Would you go and get my daughter. Get Miss Barbara to come, will you?"

She heard Hooper go out of the ladies' room and the hiss of the pneumatic door closer and after a second she opened the toilet door. The attendant had her back turned. Tess got out through the door into the hall. Now if it was *meant*—

She looked around. There was no time to consider outcomes. Quick. Either now or never. She looked wildly around and saw a door marked FIRE EXIT ONLY.

She pushed it. Ran down steps. If she could get down eighteen floors before Barbara found out . . .

* * *

Everybody said that Tess Adams came into her own when she was about twenty.

She had been acceptable; nice-looking was most frequently how she was described. Then, late-flowering, overnight she had looks, carriage, grace bestowed on her as if she had pleased hitherto indifferent gods. Why, Tizzie, Mama said, you are lovely, do you know that?

Out of a chubby-cheeked pretty but suet face emerged the longish, slant-eyed, fine-boned, thinly drawn face that was to be so admired when she was old. Out of stocky girl-scoutish colt legs emerged her well-contrived body with effective breasts that didn't protrude too much beyond being noticeable and were pointed as lemons and a curvaceous back which was enormously effective naked in a half light because of the nature of her perfect skin. All this was arranged for her without her knowledge, as it were, without any participation on her part. No creams, dieting or exercise performed this skillful mutation; it came about softly like a late spring and was suddenly there just as the first green leaf.

One would have thought this verdure would enliven her but she seemed at a loss as to how to cope with her flowering. She knew there was something missing in her which was the reason she couldn't respond properly to the boys who took her out. There was something vacant at the core of her and she fretted about what it might be; neither ecstatic nor despairing, she seemed to wander in a limbo of middling emotions and tepid desires. She felt she should have more response to the men who set out to charm her and spent energy and money doing so, and felt both sorry and a failure when she could not feel much of anything about them, neither pleasure when they arrived nor pain when they gave her up. Why can't I *feel?* She kept on and on at herself that she ought to *feel* more and small terrors passed through her, like cold ripples across a stream, that she might be frigid. She knew, just as Zina Edwards had told her years ago, she had no compassion. Therefore she wondered could this be physically related? Therefore she delayed her sexual coming out; resisted deflowering just as somebody suspecting a malignancy resists the doctor for fear of confirmation. Instead, she chose the most banal of all remedies, the trip abroad. "Go by boat," Mama said. "The first time always go by boat and anyway, there won't be any more boats soon."

First, it was too late now, beyond Sandy Hook, to discover Heather Keep was a drag of such titanic proportions it made the tongue dry to think they were going to be travel companions for seven weeks. "I'll bet a million we were the only dopes to be in our cabin when they brought the baggage and had to tip them," Heather said and then, "Oh, can they *spare* the closet space?" "Don't be taken in by all this French *politesse*," Heather said. "They want us for our dollars and they will be out to get us at every turn." "Don't look now," Heather undertoned (undertoning was one of her few gifts), "but in a minute turn around and look at what Mrs. Frank has on tonight. Oh, it's bingo night in Grand Rapids."

Secondly, the boys who heartily took up with them and bought them drinks and placed their bets on the horse racing all had *that* in mind and continually they laid *their* bets on the wrong girl so that whereas Heather let it be subtly known she might play around with a little shipboard shuffleboard (she was always ruffling the petticoats of her New Look evening dresses), they turned hungry eyes on Tess and when she tried to cool them off with humorous but tough desistance, mistook it for playing the game and increased their mute propositions, held her very close dancing, came up behind her deck chair, putting their hands over her eyes and roguishly asking her to guess who.

In order to have at least something to remember, she allowed herself to be kissed on the boat deck under a full moon, the wind blowing her hair wildly about and picking up her skirts provocatively, but the kiss went awry and their teeth gnashed together hurtfully and she said, "Didn't mean to set your teeth on edge," and it was remarks like this, getting around the boys, that left her sitting alone the last two nights before Le Havre.

There was this young man that she noticed didn't notice *her;* never asked her to dance, passed her deck chair without glancing at her. At first she thought he and the girl were a newly married couple but then, retiring one night to her cabin, came upon them kissing good night and going their separate ways. Only then it dawned on her they had identical chins, rather pronounced chins, and taking note of the girl's cabin number, looked them up on the passenger list; found they were Bracken, Nancy, U127, and Bracken, E. O., U134.

Brother and sister, they were that unique thing, one. They were never apart. They had two drinks before dinner at the same reserved table every night, never turned to look at anyone else, danced together very prettily as though they had taken an Arthur Murray course; they did fancy turns without the least affectation; they never smiled at each other or seemed to be requiring to make conversation. She grew envious of them. Once she went out of her way to go past their dining table. "Good evening," she said and they raised their similar faces to her in mild surprise and both said "Good evening" as one and turned their long aristocratic faces back to the menu.

Only once, on the very last evening on board, did she come upon Bracken, E. O., alone. He was leaning on the rail and looking out across the darkening sea as if he willed something to rise out of it and spell out some enormous meaning. He kept his cigarette in his mouth so the smoke of it, blowing into his eyes, made him seem to be weeping silently and the wind blew his soft fair hair about, so she saw it was already thinning in front to baby fuzz.

She leaned on the rail just far enough away not to seem intruding and waited while they passed across the Atlantic together for about a sea mile and then she said, "Windy," and felt like a cheap pickup (yet Heather would have said I wonder if you have a match or a lighter and could we just step out of the wind a minute) and Bracken, E. O., turned and looked at her as though she had spoken improperly during a sermon. He gave her the ghost of a smile in pity. "Yes," he said and turned and went very quickly down stairway B. It came over her in a surprise of sadness that she would never see him again in her life once they debarked.

But at least she had *felt* something.

So by the time she slipped and fell on Vesuvius it was all a miracle.

First God stepped in in Paris and sent Heather to the American Hospital and then home with mild hepatitis.

Then, thankful to be gloriously alone, she set out to enjoy Paris, picturing herself as being that slightly mysterious American girl, fancying she might even have a charming brief *alliance*. But she found it wasn't such an advantage being a mysterious American girl alone. It was difficult in restaurants. There were shrugs when they found at a peak time she wanted a table for one. They were suddenly *réservé*. She had to dine at unpopular early hours. Sitting in sidewalk cafés, she became aware of the stares by men (and once on the Left Bank by an interested girl) and the slight moving of chairs nearer unnerved her, so she gripped her book and pretended to read. She would get so nervous she would have to ask for the bill and leave and then have nowhere to go except back to the hotel. She asked for her key so often that the concierge took to sighing. "You do not enjoy Paris, M'd'moiselle?" he asked when on the third evening in a row she was home by nine-thirty. "Oh, yes, *mais oui,*" she said, "but I am busy—*très occupe,*" she said and made the miming of writing, writing.

"Dommage," he said.

Once she caught sight of the Brackens in the Louvre. They had on similar windbreakers and identical little Harris tweed caps. "Hello," she said gaily. "We were on the same ship." They nodded to her but were absorbed in reading their catalogue.

She hurried through streets exquisitely designed for dawdling as though she were late for an important assignation. Her competent French deserted her. "Um—um—*je vous en prie—que—*er—" she stumbled. Then, reaching the safety of her room, looked at her hollow disappointed face in the mirror, felt desolate.

She moved on. In Venice she thought she looked incongruous in a gondola alone. When she tried lolling back against the cushions, she felt a severe crick in her neck and also ludicrous and the gondolier kept muttering fiercely to her and calling out (she suspected) cantankerous things about her to the other *gondolieri.* Late at night, crossing the empty Piazza San Marco, she heard an Italian voice cry from the shadows of the dark porticoes, "Hellooo," and again, softly and caressingly, "Helloooooo," and when panic shot through her and she darted off, heels clicking, the voice called, "Why are you so afraid?" In the emptiness of the columns the word followed her like smoke. *Afraaaid.*

In Rome an attractive young Englishman spoke to her in the Piazza Navona on the night she was sitting among the beauties of lighted stone and shimmering waters and contemplating going home. She allowed him to buy her a negroni and, released after so long from her prison of silence, conversation and gaiety flowed from her until he rose to greet his date, a haughty English girl, and minutes later murmured apologies that they had reservations some-where. She ordered another negroni and resolutely told herself she must stick it out even if only to try to test her endurance, and being lonely beyond words, her skin paining with forlornness and something close to self-pity, felt she might find alone what was missing in herself. So she walked the ruins, hugging her wistful contemplation around her shoulders; stared into the dark, deserted Forum. Felt a degree of strength in this sort of self-cauterizing of the ego. It was very late when she got back to the hotel and she had to ring for the night porter. Then, try as she might, she could not get her door to unlock. She wrestled with the giant key this way and that, making as much noise in the silent hall as if she were opening a postern gate to admit the regiment. Down she had to go for the night porter, who came up and opened the door for her and smiled. He was young and quite beautiful. He looked at her very directly with enormous sad eyes and for a split second she had the insane desire to kiss him. Instead she fumbled in her bag for a tip. *"Multo grazie,"* she said. *"Prego,"* he said and smiled at her. He was as lonely as she, his look had told her; he completely understood. What if she had been made love to for the first time in life by a lonely Italian night porter? But well-brought-up American girls don't do things like that. Besides, she said, opening the shutters to the night, his bell might have rung. Just the same, she said, I got a message from him.

Then she fell on Vesuvius and was caught by Mr. Bracken.

Looking down into the ghastliness of this monumental ashtray, the horror of the walls of gray ash, the sea of ash they told her was miles deep, her fear of heights, the dreadful silence, the wisps of smoke coming from the sides, hanging onto the boulder, she slipped and slid down the incline, grazing her knees, and rolled toward the cinder path and was picked up by Elton Bracken. "Oh," she gasped. "Fancy. We came over together on the ship," she said, being picked up, and stared at, and incidentally photographed by a fat man from Racine, Wisconsin.

"Are you hurt?" Mr. Bracken asked. His sister, Nancy, was offering her a handkerchief and because of all the little torments and snubs and lonely nights and misunderstandings over language and tips, she wept and wept. They sat her on a stone and Nancy dabbed

95

at her bleeding knees and Elton stood and blinked at her.

"Oh, please, I'm all right," she sobbed and went into another paroxysm because it felt so delightful and to hell with the tourists looking at her being such a ninny over a slight accident and carrying on so.

"Are you staying in Naples?" she hiccuped. "I feel such an idiot but—everything has been going wrong." The Brackens stood beside her, looking discomforted but compassionate, while she finished out her attack of hysterics. She found herself blurting out that she had hated *hated* her trip, that everything had gone wrong, the car not here *here*, the train *there* no longer on the schedule given her in New York, the horrid French, the ghastly Venetians, "and I haven't had a poached egg for *weeks*," she wailed unreasonably.

Beyond the wildest of hopes, the Brackens were staying (not surprisingly, because the town was tiny) in the same hotel as she in Resina and she found herself with them at nightfall having Camparis in a dusty little street bar, delighted at donkeys and beautiful Italian peasants. Most of all, delighted with the Brackens. "I don't think—" one would begin and the other would take up and finish the sentence. Elton was going to Harvard Law School and Nancy "didn't do anything." Their parents were dead. There was something ineffably gentle about them and reassuring.

They all went to Pompeii together and walking the cobbled streets Tess felt she had known them forever.

"In case you'd like to know, Tess," Elton began, "about the bricks," Nancy said, "this is the reticulated diamond-shaped brick from the age of Augustine," Elton said.

"And this, Tess," Nancy said, "is the more modern kind of brick from about the time of Nero."

"Is this getting to be a bore for you?" Elton asked.

"Oh, *no.*"

"Because if it's a bore—"

"—say so," the Brackens said in tune.

"There's nothing worse," Nancy began, "than dragging somebody who isn't as interested as us," Elton went on, "through Pompeii," Nancy ended.

Sometimes she let them walk a step ahead of her because it was touching to watch the way he treated his sister as though she were eggshell, his hand constantly under her elbow, assisting her with obsolete courtesy over the merest step, slightest corner.

"Imagine," he began. "They had warning days before."

"Days before," Nancy echoed. "Imagine. The earthquake came first before the eruption, which took place—"

"—we think on a Friday," Elton said.

They stood in the windy forum and the Brackens described as though they had been there the vast plume of smoke, the eerie rumblings, the hot winds blowing, the beginning of the tide of cinders cascading in blazing light in the night. "All around here they ran, ran, dragging what they could with them."

"Oh, I love it," Tess said. "Why is it we love to be on the site of disasters?"

"It makes us feel immortal," Elton said and gave her a gentle smile and straightened his little Harris tweed cap. At the same moment Nancy straightened hers.

Then, from a tower, they looked out on yellow fields of millet where women dressed in blue skirts harvested with scythes.

"Oh, I love it," Tess cried out. "I love it, the whole thing. I love *everything.*"

They tapped on her door just as she was going to bed. "Were you just going to bed?" they asked her. "Come into Elton's room for a minute. We want to show you something."

There, they said, look. The lights of Naples twinkled to the right. Way to the left, the fainter lights of Capri winked. Toward Sorrento fireworks flashed and burst in the night sky under the moon.

"We seem to be—" Elton said, "—surfeited tonight," Nancy said.

The Brackens leaned one each side of her out the window, the night wind stirring their finely thin hair and their jutting aristocratic chins and similar noses, and Tess was so in love with them both she felt burnished with pride and honor. They were so attractive, so civilized, so nice, so American. They were the perfect American prototype. Had she the power, she would recommend to Congress that the Brackens be packaged in some way and sent around the world as living disputation of the canard that all Americans are aggressive, loud-mouthed, vulgar and greedy.

"I just love everything," she said. Most of all I love you two. Oh, God, she said, kneeling and looking up at the dark hulk of Vesuvius, "or whoever's listening, thank you for making me slip but oh, *God,* keep it going, will you? Don't let it be one of those ships-passing-in-the-night things."

There are more than a dozen tunnels between Naples and Rome through which the train twists and turns under mountains, and in their compartment the lights had not been turned on so they were rushed in and out of daylight and blackness, but it was comforting the way the Brackens continued to talk in the dark, reassuring, as they went on, completely unconcerned with being made bodiless, their voices never varying in tone, only lifting slightly over the noise of the train rushing through a tunnel. Once in the dark Elton said, "Are you looking at me, Tess?" Her heart nearly fell out on the floor and she laughed at the image of the Brackens, so polite and thoughtful, bending over the train floor to find her dropped heart.

They sat in the cool of the Roman night in the garden of that Alberto's which is in the shadow of a great church; they had the huge shrimps with whiskers, "like Teddy Roosevelt," they said. Around them, the endless traffic of Rome hummed and honked. But suddenly an argument had flared into a fight close by them on the street. A man and woman screaming at each other in a violent way, arms and heads waving, fists clenched, an Italian falling-out. Tess noticed it distressed Elton very much. He had stood up and his face was in pain, his mouth sucked up in pain. "Oh, they shouldn't," Elton said. He was actually physically appalled by violence, Tess thought, and thought at the same time that *she* felt nothing particular about it, any

98

more than one would in New York City; only that it was ugly and disagreeable. The woman spat in the man's face and then he hit her bluntly in the mouth with his fist and a tiny driblet of blood ran out of her mouth no bigger than a few drops of wine but Elton gave a cry and ran down the steps and pulled the man away and said in a severe way, "No, you must *never* hit a woman." So, typically, the man and woman united, turned on him in a burst of furious invective while he stood there shaking his head at them sorrowfully, and then the woman spat at his feet and said something and then with scorn, *"Americano."* Elton came back to the table in a resigned way and for the first time Tess heard Nancy disavow their Siamese unanimity. "You shouldn't interfere," Nancy said.

It led somehow to talk about the nature of people.

"People are basically good," Nancy said. "I believe that."

"Basically," Elton said, "people are good. I'm old-fashioned. I believe basically good wins out in the end."

"In the end," Nancy said. "That's why I think *we'll* always get through. America, I mean."

"Will get through," Elton said, "because in spite of all the villains and nuts and cranks, the majority of Americans are good. I don't think anything will ever happen to us like—"

"—Hitler," Nancy said.

"No, people are basically good," the Brackens said in unison and Tess felt it was so if the Brackens said it was.

Oh, don't stay *there,* the Brackens had said when they had arrived back in Rome. It's too big and commercial. No *wonder* you weren't crazy about Rome. We always stay at the Nazionale; it's cheap and besides, it's on the old square where the city hall is and all the *carabinieri* are there in scarlet and black and with their Napoleon hats. She felt by now accepted by them and truly, Rome seemed different, smiling; the azaleas tumbled down the Spanish Steps in waterfalls. "Oh, *bellissima,"* Tess said.

One little odd thing happened. She had impulsively bought a blue dish for Nancy on the Via Sistina and when she knocked on Nancy's door there was a pause and Elton said, "Who is it?" He opened the door a crack and said in a tense way, "Yes?" and Tess could see Nancy lying on the bed, her face turned away from the door. "A little pretty thing I saw in a window," Tess said. "Isn't Nancy feeling well?" He seemed so strange, was she intruding on some private drama? "Oh, there's nothing wrong; no, she's fine," Elton said; took the gift coldly as if it were a summons. "Thank you, Fran," he said and then, *"Tess,* I mean. We know a girl named Fran; sorry." Well, see you later, Tess said but he had already shut the door quickly in her face.

Then at six her phone jingled arthritically and Elton said, "Tess, we're just going to have a quiet dinner in the room tonight so—" "Oh, perfectly all right," she lied. "It'll give me a chance to get together with this friend of my mother's." It was strange how bereft she felt, thinking of the whole long evening without them. Some family upset? Quarrel? Just seemed out of the question they could have a falling-out.

But bright and early next morning Nancy phoned to say she loved the dish, how sweet of you, Tess. Did you have a nice evening? Where did you and your mother's friend dine? Oh, she wasn't? Oh, what a pity. Oh, we should have warned you not to go *there;* it's the biggest gyp in Rome. What a drag; we had business. Listen, let's go buy prosciutto and cheese and wine and—and (Elton took the phone) have a picnic maybe in the Baths of Caracalla. You haven't seen it.

On the last day before the Brackens were to fly home, in a sunny square, waiting while Elton bought a new roll of film, Nancy said, "Elton likes you, Tess."

Again she felt lifted up.

"Do you like him?" Nancy asked.

"Oh, Nancy, I adore you *both."*

"Yes, but do you like *him?"*

"Oh, *yes."*

Nancy sat down on a ledge and stared away. "He's very good and sweet, really," she said.

"Oh, I know."

"He's the dearest thing, really."

She went with them to the *stazione* to catch their airport bus. "I'm in the Manhattan book," she said desperately. "I'm on Thirtieth near Lexington and I'll be in and out most of the summer and then *most* of the time here all winter because I'm going to take a course at the New School," she said urgently, despairingly, as if they were being deported to New Zealand.

They waved through the bus window. They flattened their noses against the glass like children. Then they were gone in a cloud of blue exhaust.

Rome was again sullen and gray; she was poured on by a sudden rain and once more petrified of crossing the Piazza di Spagna against the traffic. "Always try to cross with nuns," the Brackens had told her.

They didn't phone.

Their number in New Jersey never answered. Still, her hopes leapt whenever hers rang.

Then in July Mama called from Bedford.

"Was it a Nancy Bracken you met in Italy? Well, she's dead. It's in the *Times*."

BRACKEN—Nancy Elizabeth, on July 17. Beloved daughter of the late Ormond and Ellen (née Fownes) Bracken of Foothills, New Jersey, and dearly loved sister of Elton Ormond. Funeral private.

Dear Elton (she wrote), I cannot seem to find the— Dearest Elton, In what must be this terrible hour— My dear Elton, My deepest most tender loving heartbroken condolences go out to you, dear, dear friend at this—

Finally she wrote, "Elton, If and when you feel you want to talk to someone, I am here. Tess."

He came up the stairs, thinner.

"Hello."

"Tess. I'm a bit early."

"Right on time, Elton. Hello."

"Hello. I walked."

"From where?"

"Harvard Club."

"Is that where you're staying?"

"Uh-huh. This is nice, Tess."

"Sublet. Let me have your coat."

"Roomy and a fireplace."

"Doesn't work and I don't care much for her taste in . . ." Trying not to let him see she was stricken with the looks of him, so thin and something in the eyes that tended to make you avoid looking into them. He was like someone recuperating from a long serious illness.

"Now what may I get you?"

"Oh, I don't know, Tess. Anything at all, thank you."

"Gin? Scotch? Vodka?"

"I haven't been drinking at *all* lately; I'm afraid those might put me on my ear. Would you have any just plain white wine?"

"Oh, I don't think—let me look. I don't *think*—it didn't occur to me—"

"Oh, look, don't mind—just plain tonic water."

"With nothing in it?"

"Nothing in it."

So difficult to avoid any reference to their past, to Italy, to anything that might remind him, and on the other hand having nothing much else to talk about. And he sitting politely and his neck so thin sticking out of his shirt collar and his jaw jutting forward, which even in gladder times gave him the melancholy look of a marsh bird.

"Went to the Koussevitzky the other night," she informed him.

"Was it good?"

"Marvelous. Mahler."

"Is that so?"

"Ravel."

Driplets of talk and her voice high-pitched and forced-sounding, like an ingenue in some play introduced only to set up the major characters; also the lump in her throat of pity for him. She had never experienced, even with Daddy's death, grief as deep as his; never seen a young man so robbed. When he looked around the room from time to time, at this, at that, it was as if he were looking for Nancy.

"Except the Russian Tea Room's always so jam packed and they put you at those little tables so close together I always feel a sort of claustro—"

"Yes."

"And such a lot of sour cream on everything."

"I prefer simple food. In fact, I'm rather dull about food."

"That's good, because all you're going to get tonight is meatballs and spaghetti. I've been very badly brought up, you see."

"That's just what would suit me."

"Now, are you sure you won't let me put just a drop of gin in it this time?"

"No, thank you, Tess."

"And how've you—is it going at law school?"

"It's been—oh, I persevere."

How could she break through to him? She was aching to suddenly run across the room and put her arms around this thin creature and say who's looking after you? Who can you talk to? What can *I* be to you?

Then she achieved it with a small blunder. "Cookies?" she said, holding out the dish, which he took and examined and said, "This's the same dish you gave Nancy, isn't it?"

"Yes." Damn. "I bought two. In the Via Sistina."

He held the blue dish as if waiting to be given communion and she waited, knowing they were suddenly gathered together in the cathedral of his loss. After a long while, he cleared his throat and said, addressing the cookies, "Tess, we knew, you know, in Europe. We knew."

"I see."

"She wanted to see France and Italy once more. But we knew all the time she only had about two or three months at the outside."

"Ah."

"So wasn't she marvelous? Would you ever have guessed anything at all?"

"Not in a million—"

"Wasn't she marvelous? Well, in a way that's what's helped pull me through, thinking how marvelous she was even in the bad times, like the night you brought the dish to her room and she was so ill."

"I wouldn't have known, thought you might have had bad news from home or something."

"Well, she was very ill that night, one of the bad times. All she ever said was, 'I hate to be so dull.' But anyway, that's that. So if I can, I want to try to remember her joy."

"Oh, yes, oh, that's nice, Elton."

"What's so difficult is she was the outgoing side of me. I'm not very *out*going."

"Yes."

"And it's as if I'd lost my voice because so often I would *think* the thing and she would *say* it."

Well, it wasn't going to be good enough to pity him and pity is an ungraceful thing and fortunately fleeting. But it wasn't enough, she thought, watching out the window as he went up the windy street and paused uncertainly at the corner, looking this way and that, as if not sure which way was uptown.

But something was begun.

Would Tess mind if his cousin Willis joined them? And if cousin Willis was all he had to fall back on he was even more to be pitied. Cousin Willis wore a massive silver stag's head on a chain from which sharp antlers sprouted as if to safeguard her from any physical contact. "Better let *me* check the check," cousin Willis said. "They only have to *look* at you to know you're the easiest take in town." "Elton thinks the best of *everyone*," cousin Willis said witheringly, "and this is the man who's going to be the great *lawyer*."

"Listen," Tess said, heart palpitating but trying to make it sound as though she had just thought of it that minute. "Would you and cousin Willis come up to Bedford for Thanksgiving and maybe stay over the—"

"Oh, not *Willie,* Tess," he said, appalled. "Would you mind? I mean, is it—would it be all right if just *I* came?"

"Well," Mama said to him, "imagine you knowing the Fitzroy Candells. One of the boys married a schoolmate of mine in Coleville, Pennsylvania, where I'm from."

"They were the Westport side," Elton said. "We only knew the *Phillip* Fitzroy side. They were I think from the *Nyack* side."

"Oh, Honoria."

"Yes, exactly."

"Then she was originally a Bannock."

"Right, ma'am. And it was *Hugh* Bannock, who'd be her brother's son, who was—um—going to be engaged to my sister."

"Oh, I see."

"And *his* sister, Cornelia, married Drum Candell of the *other* Candell family."

"They were what? Mining? Yes, and Delia—Diddle we called her —had two daughters who were great beauties."

"Right, ma'am. Geraldine, and I forget the other one's name."

"Geraldine," Mama said, "was first married to a Wyatt and divorced him and married Prince Rondanini, who had been married to Elena Rothschild."

"The other girl," Elton said, "became a drunk."

"Oh," Mama said, "poor thing."

He kissed Tess for the first time under a winter tree. It was rather like being kissed behind the coatrack at the school dance. Then, "Was it all right, me doing that?"

"Elton," she said, at a loss.

"What?"

"I wish I had an outgoing person to speak for *me* too. About what I think."

"But I'm not intruding on anything, am I?"

"No, Elton, you're not."

At dinner he raised his glass and said, "May I make a toast? To my . . . rescuers."

"Why, that's very sweet," Mama said. "Very sweet indeed, Elton."

Mama leaned in the doorway. Tess was propped up in bed, reading.

"Is this—is this anything?"

"Anything?"

Mama sat down on the bed. "Serious."

"I don't know, Mama. Not yet anyway."

"Tiz, he's just as nice as he can be; a dear boy, I think."

"Yes, he is."

"*I* think. Beautiful old-fashioned manners and deeply sincere. I think he's very suitable."

"Suitable! What a vile word."

"Well, I didn't mean it in the sense of—"

"Suitable—how horrible. It makes me cringe. *Suit*able."

"Tess—"

"And I know why. Because it's right. Yes, yes, it's right, the right kind of word for me. I'm the kind of girl who will probably make a *suitable* marriage because I'm—"

"Oh, dear, *Tiz,* I didn't mean to upset you this way—"

"Suitable." She threw her pillow across the room and bit on her lip and gasped to stop the tears.

"I just feel there must—ought to be something better than suitable, Mama, that's all, and I don't know why I can't seem to find it. I don't know."

"I didn't know either that you were sensitive about this—feeling this way about yourself, Tiz, which is, I ab-so-lute-ly assure you, one hundred percent wrong—"

"*May*be."

"One hundred percent—"

"We'll see."

"I wish you'd think how lovely you are for a—"

"Never mind, Mama. You are right, maybe. We'll see."

"What can I say to you, Tess, to make you—"

"You don't have to say *anything.* I'm sorry I blew up."

Mama hesitated, one hand on the china doorknob, the other to her forehead. Forgotten something; what was it? Blinked at the floor. *Oh,* yes.

"No matter what you think, I'm interested in you."

"Mama, why do you even *say* that?"

"Well, just . . . once in a blue moon, occasionally . . . I feel a little bit guilty, you see, that it was Daddy you lost, not me."

Now she wasn't the kind of girl could scramble out of bed, rush and squeeze and kiss and assure; could only mumble Mother weakly, tch tch tch, she said, oh, *really.* But she was appalled at her inability; it was like opening a drawer and finding something horribly dead in it.

But maybe suitable wasn't so bad. She'd read and heard that good marriages are often made without passion and who was she, after all, to expect and demand things she didn't seem capable of returning. *Fondness* she could give, Oh, she was overwhelmed with fondness for him, occasionally mixed with the feeling of fright, sometimes weariness at the thought of all this valuableness being offered her (Was it all right, me doing that?), sweetness that was sometimes damned hard to bear. Like *there* he was, wouldn't you know, not waiting inside the warm lobby like any sensible man would on a night when it was fourteen degrees and a knifelike wind blowing down Fifty-seventh Street (and what *any* New Yorker can tell you is that outside Carnegie Hall is the coldest spot south of the North Pole *always*) and there he was, in his cap, his muffler blowing around in the icy wind, tears of cold running down his face, hands in pockets, dancing up and down in his suede boots on the frozen sidewalk, watching out for her, anguished (she drew into a doorway for a second to watch him, both frightened and touched by the look on his face), turning first this way, then that, then bending low to see who was this in the cab, was this her at last? She was very late. He looked at his watch, he danced in the cold, he craned his long neck to see over people's heads. Where was she? Ill? Forgetful? Not coming? His anguished face said, peering anxiously in despair at each woman approaching, if she did not come he would be absolutely lost. But he would wait for her in the bitter cold until the damn concert was over and the last person left and they put out the lights and that was the kind of person he was.

"Oh, Elton," she said, and grabbed him. "You darling, you idiot, why didn't you wait in the warm *lobby?* What can I *do* about you?"

"Cold," he said, "is bracing for the skin. Don't you want me to have nice firm skin when I'm old?"

He took off her mittens and rubbed her cold hands in his.

"Here's a picture of a funny Boston horse," he wrote on a postcard. "Exams, exams. E."

He wrote, "No getting down to NY; the insolence of office and the law's delay (Hamlet). E." Two extremely tentative kisses had been appended at the bottom. She began obscurely accepting it; she began feeling curiously settled. It was restful. She might as well put on, as the song says, a happy face. She put on a face of love, put on a Giaconda smile and felt smug and at peace as if she had eaten a comb of honey.

She walked the streets of New York smiling with her peace and causing old ladies to say to each other that how sad, that beautiful young girl is a little insane.

Two words smashed all this to pieces like glass.

"Drop by," Lacey said.

And although Lacey was renowned for giving parties that were unequaled in whimsy and discomfort, she went.

Lacey was wearing a floor-length black satin dress and a long molting feather boa, almost black lipstick and she had moistened her hair into little spit curls of queries.

Maybe she had found the guests through the Yellow Pages. Lacey never introduced anyone. There was only red wine and cheese and hard peaches for which no knives were provided.

And Lacey seemed to be in a sour mood.

It would have only been ten minutes at the outside before Tess would have left, after wandering around, sitting here and there, eavesdropping on the elusive knots of conversation. She answered two questions—"Is there any Liederkranz?" and "Are you Lew

Mandel's girl?"—with the same answer. "I don't think so."

Ten minutes earlier and she would have been off and away.

"Oh, God, look at him," a girl screamed.

What? Everyone turned. People got up off the floor. There was a rush toward somebody who had just come in. Tess could not see anything but people's backs.

"Get a towel," somebody said.

"Crush up some ice," somebody said.

"Ugh, I can't look," a girl said.

"But how did it happen?"

"What is it?" Tess asked.

She craned her neck to glimpse over shoulders the blond young man they crowded around. He was holding something up to his face.

"Slashed."

"How?"

"Lacey, there's no *ice.*"

Suddenly she was right beside him. His blue eyes looked up. He was extraordinarily good-looking and a fearful wound ran from just above his chin to the ear.

He was saying he never saw who it was, someone ran out of a dark doorway and just—he didn't even feel it at first.

"Oh, how brutal," somebody said.

Lacey seemed Orientally unconcerned. "How about an aspirin?" she said.

"Aspirin!" Tess turned angrily on her. "Call an ambulance; he should have that stitched at once."

"New York Hospital's quickest," someone said.

"How about a Band-Aid?" Lacey said.

"Leeches," the young man said. "You always have plenty around." He peeled off the "wound," realistically made of plastic. It was one of those novelties that so delight the less sophisticated in Times Square.

"Ham!"

"Ham, you gook."

The young man was laughing and brushing his untidy blond hair off his face; he had a perfect beauty spot on one cheek. Or maybe that came off too.

Oh, Ham, they said, you are the end. Hamilton, a girl said, you ought not to get laid for a week, you are so evil. That would teach you to go around scaring people.

"Oh, don't pay him any attention," Lacey said. "His need for attention is super psychotic."

"Who is he?" Tess asked.

"Ham Hoban. You've met him."

"Never."

"Sure you have. He's a Canadian. Photographer."

"Never," Tess said. "I would have remembered."

"Don't have anything to do with him," Lacey said and narrowed her eyes. "He's dangerous."

"How?"

"He'd eat *you* up."

"Why me especially?" She was getting annoyed at Lacey's attitude, which seemed to presuppose her virginity.

"Because you are a sincere girl, Tess."

That made her grab a glass of wine and stay and hope the beautiful young man would come up and say something to her and she would be both disdainful and seductive. But he stayed away, head and shoulders above everyone else in the room, looking, with his untidy blond hair and blue sailor pants, like a golden-skinned Scandinavian sailor who'd jumped ship.

So after a desultory conversation with a cynical Englishman from the UN, she went into the bedroom and got her coat and bag.

"Running off?"

He was blocking the door.

"I'm Ham Hoban. Who are you?"

She told him.

"Where are you in such a hurry to get to on a Sunday evening? Church?"

He would be about six feet four and he obviously enjoyed it.

"Have a glass of redeye," he said, handing her one of two glasses he had been holding as if waiting for someone. "I've been watching you," he said. "Why do you move about so much?"

"I?"

"A girl like you should stand perfectly still and let them come to *you*. There isn't a girl in the room to hold a candle to you."

The best thing certainly was to be still about these compliments. He was very practiced at this sort of thing obviously; this was his line, this old stuff.

"You should just stand still and let them come to you."

She just stared him out.

"Why are you so nervous?" The beauty spot was in the exact right place. It was tiresome in a way, this excessive handsomeness, boring as a soap ad. So why did she keep staring at him the way he wanted her to and why was she unaccountably caught up in a wind and blown around?

"I'm not nervous, just bored," she said.

"Getting up, sitting down, grinning at all those nobodies, overeager—"

"I'm not; I'm being normally polite—"

"Look at you now, look the way you're holding your redeye and your bag. I'm not going to snatch it."

True, she was all hunched up against the wall as if it were the subway and he was a hulking bag snatcher.

"A wow like you shouldn't be all tied up in knots. What's your problem?"

"I happen—Mr. Hoban, is it?—not to be tied up in knots."

Oh, she sounded so put-on, prim, snooty Bennington girl flirting with a beau. Because she was excited, it was crystal clear he suspected she was a virgin; something in the look he gave her, which was half suspecting, half incredulous.

"Oh, well," he said and made a slight move away and she thought he's going, that's the end of that, and fell down a hole into the earth and soared up again when he said, "I'm naturally curious about people and I am curious about you."

"Oh," she said, "I'm terrifically mundane."

He was even better looking when he was no longer smiling.

"Why'd you come this evening?" he asked as if it were important.

"Why? I'm a friend of Lacey's, that's all."

"Do you go everyplace you're invited?"

"Not at all."

"I bet you didn't want to come this evening but you didn't have anything else to do."

But she would not fall into that easy trap of pretty denial, pretended indignation. That would do for the other girls, who must have tossed indignant delighted heads at him; heads tumbled before him by the hundred, she knew that. He was the supreme poseur-egotist. She sipped Lacey's hot strong wine. *Seemed* hot, warmed up at least, the way it lit up her stomach.

"Do you wear gray a lot?" he asked.

"Is this a personality analysis?" she asked. Only the cheap wine made it come out "alanysis."

"I bet you do wear gray a lot, beige, dull colors."

"What does it matter?"

He put a finger on her chin and wiped away a spot of wine. "You know why? Because gray makes you disappear into it and you feel safer."

Poseur, provocateur, and the thrilling and disastrous thing about him was he gave you the impression he just might be sincere.

And she felt sensually flattered from head to toe.

That's why she stayed still, not moving an inch. That's why, with her adrenaline going like electrolysis through her and the wine going to her head and her feet nailed to the floor.

The long-avoided thing was here. The forces of counterattraction had brought it right to her and she felt certain if she avoided it again it would somehow affect the rest of her life. There was a spooky kind of inevitability about it, standing with this man in a narrow little hall, having just met; yet she was as sure of it as of anything in her life and the feeling was like being hurtled upward in an express elevator and it made her dizzier than the wine. She couldn't take in what Ham was saying and so she tried deep breathing and leaned on a bookcase for support and locked her knees to prevent them from buckling the way she'd heard that horses do to sleep standing up.

Because it was fascinating, unthinkable, extraordinary to think she might actually be going to . . . and the thought of it crossing her mind this way and that obliterated all thoughts of what anyone might think. And besides, he made it so easy.

"I'm sick of this," he said, putting down his wine. "Shall we go?"

It was a big bare photographer's studio with a bed on the floor. On one wall was a huge blowup of one of his nude studies. On the other wall was a huge golden letter *S*.

She sat on a leather pouf and allowed him to get her a large vodka and admired his skylight. Talk spilled out of her.

"I'm very self-contained," she told him. "I'm very self-sufficient, no matter what you may think. It's been my drawback in many ways. At school, for instance, I wasn't popular because everybody thought I was a snob. I wasn't a snob at all; I just had very strong preconceptions of my own. I've always been very *assured*," she said.

"My father gave me this self-assurance. 'For God's sake, have an opinion of your own and stick to it,' he said and I have, ever since I was thirteen, and I think possibly it's the greatest gift he gave me —that self-*reliance* that so many people think is coldness on my part. You'd be surprised how many people think oh, Tess Adams is a cold fish, when all the time it is just that I can't bend my opinions to them if I don't have the—"

She couldn't go on. His silence was thunderous.

"That is a pack of lies," she said.

Probably from the excitement of this confession, she plunged to the other extreme; pulled herself to pieces. I am vodka-izing, she thought, but to pour it out to him was voluptuous. She told about the night in Venice when the soft voice had called out to her from the shadows, Why are you so afraid? Why are you so afraaaid? She imitated the voice. Ham had taken a pair of nail scissors to his hands.

Maybe she'd mishandled it. Maybe it wasn't going to happen after all. What a marvelous jawline he had. He was no longer interested in her. She had bungled it. Oh, well. She looked at his nude girl on the wall and the nude girl looked back at her; it was highly unlikely that *she* had thrown away her chance.

Snip, snip went the nail scissors.

She said, "Did you know there are two Statues of Liberty in New York? One day I was walking in the West Sixties and I looked up and there on the roof of a dingy old building was this Statue of Liberty. I guess hardly anyone knows she's there—hardly anyone looks up and sees her and yet someone went to all the trouble of having her made and putting her there and was so proud of her. Well, sometimes I feel like *her,* holding my torch there, year after year, and nobody bothering to look up and see me."

"What do you intend to do about it?"

"I don't know."

"For a start why don't you stop hiding in that gray dress?" he said and, leaning over, began to unbutton her.

Well, it was such a sense of deep well-being and fulfillment that she was afraid to move in case it shattered; well, it had been (if she were being asked to describe it into microphones at an airport) "beyond her wildest dreams." Even the awkward, slightly painful beginning, and now there on the floor in a streak of sunlight through slats lay her gray dress all rumpled up and after today she would never wear it again because she had shed it; it was her pupa that she had struggled out of at last from insect into butterfly freedom. She was released. She had had to restrain herself from saying to him "Thank you" when he had kissed her for the last time and turned over. She had lain on her back in the dark listening to his regular breathing and wondered if this feeling of elevation would last. Now, opening her eyes, she felt for the pulse of her spirit and found it still there, elated. Turning, she saw a wall of naked back next to her. She had the urge to put her face gently next to it but she didn't know the rules that should be followed for mornings after and how dreadful if it was the wrong thing to do and how shattering if he awoke and reared up and said who the hell are you or something.

Exultation at being finally a woman was one thing but it couldn't overcome thirst and she craved water and so extricated herself from the bed as delicately as if she were the thinnest airmail paper being slipped from the envelope so as not to disturb him.

Well (seeing herself drinking deep and thirstily from his blue cup in the bathroom mirror), it wasn't true that it didn't show; what a spinster's shibboleth *that* was. She was not the same girl who had gone last night to a party, made up of wire coat hangers under the gray dress; it was mostly a change around the mouth, a tinge of maturity and assurance, and allowing herself the vanity, she smiled and thought she probably was as lovely as some people had said. Today she was. She might never again be as lovely in her entire life but in Ham's bathroom on this day of our Lord in the 1950s she was.

Not knowing the rules for mornings after, she thought the wisest course would be not to be found; to be gone, no note, nothing cute, just gone.

As she tiptoed across the room to get her shoes, he stirred and without opening his eyes said into the pillow, "Can you get home all right?"

Well, what did it matter? (Heavens, where was she? Where *is* this? Saint *Luke's* Place?) Young gods from Parnassus who come occasionally down to parties on East Sixty-third Street and take a young maiden cannot be expected to be immaculate; they are gods. So what did she expect from him? Hail to thee, blithe spirit? Well, why pretend about it? What she would have liked from him would have been two words: "Don't go." Because "Can you get home all right" indicated no possibility of seeing him again.

(On a postcard of Cambridge Square Elton wrote, "Found the book you wanted in secondhand shop here—hope be with you week of 25th. Hope you O.K.")

To everything there is a rhyme and a reason and the reason for Ham Hoban had been what happened; it had been accomplished and that was all it was meant to be. That was that.

And the watched phone never rings.

Twice she ran frantically back upstairs all fingers and thumbs with keys and hysteria only to find it was her neighbor's phone. Once she went three stops too far on the subway and she was always catching sight of a tall blond young man head and shoulders above the crowd but not Ham.

Only once more, she said to herself; once more with him and she wouldn't ask anything more. Once more even if only to find perhaps it was anticlimactic, if only to see that incredible face and perhaps find it was not incredible at all, dumbly handsome, quickly tired of. But days and days passing with nothing in them. So why be strangely comforted when they called to say her phone was out of order? All Murray Hill 6 lines, the phone company told her. There was trouble in a cable. How long they couldn't say, madam. The phone company asked did she have an extension? One? Do not attempt to dial out or answer the telephone, the company said; it is dangerous because (a mass of technical terms), a voltage wire or something had run amok, they were warning all Murray Hill sixers. They would let her know when it was fixed. But how will I know when it's *you?* A tall young man with blond hair would come personally to tell her, the phone company said, laughing.

"Oh," she said and then to hide her elation, sternly, "Oh, are you one of those sophomoric people who like to play pranks on the phone?"

And when he came into her small room, immense in a sheepskin coat, she thought indeed there *is* something a little insane about him. He's too rich in looks and in personality, he's too big and too everything. You would be a fool to get in deep in this, she told herself in her tiny kitchen because he'd erratically asked for cocoa.

He wouldn't sit down; he roamed about, cocoa in hand, peering down at things from his great height and asking, "Is this your father?" "Who's this guy with you?"

"A boy I met in Italy."

"I thought you'd *call,*" he said. "I had to call whosis to get your number."

"Who?"

"Lacey."

She took a cigarette from a box and he came over with a lighter but took the cigarette from her mouth and kissed her and said, "You have snowballed on me."

One day hot, one day cold. There was no diagram to him. Sometimes all warmth, sometimes all chill. There was no contentment, only euphoria and implausibility, with periods of falling away, returning to sanity. Her girl friends noted she had lost weight, her mother asked about circles under her eyes. The way he could drain you. Half the time she fell into her bed and instant sleep, the other half she tossed all night. The energy of him; he was always pulling her along somewhere. Where are we going? You'll see. But whoever said there had to be contentment? Only old people surely, left with nothing else, or people who were not able to bear such emotion continuously (and they would stop and kiss on stairs, not waiting to get into her apartment, or in the hallway of his; even in Bloomingdale's) or stand the midnight calls when often there were long pauses with only a word or two said and his questions. Why did you frown then? Why did you say that? Why are you frightened of exploring yourself? Occasionally solicitous. Did you get home all right? I was worried when you didn't answer. Would you rather we didn't tonight?

She felt twinges of shame at the sense of priority it gave her to see girls notice him and turn their heads to him on the street with faintly grieving envy.

And games. Now we'll pretend I'm trying to pick you up. Pretend we're from out of town and ask someone the way to the Ritz Carlton. But they tore it down. Yes, and we'll be cut to the heart to hear it.

She worried about telling Elton. She didn't tell him and then worried about not telling him. Elton's weekend in New York was not a success. And while they were having dinner the manageress came up and said, "Miss Adams? Well, you're wanted on the phone. You can take it over there in the hat check room."

She made shrugging motions to Elton.

"What are you doing at the Washington Irving Inn? It sounds very bogus. Are there Early American prints and candles in pewter?"

"How did you know where—"

"You told me this chappie from Harvard likes to go either there or the Women's Exchange."

"Oh, yes, I did."

"I already tried the Women's Exchange. Now what kind of a man would want to go to the Women's Exchange or the Washington Irv—"

"What did you want?"

"—ing *Inn*. I bet he wears galoshes and a muffler his sister knit for him. I imagine he likes prune whip too. What are you doing wasting your—"

"Ham."

"What?"

"*I* said what. What do you want?"

"I want you."

"Ham, I—"

"I need you. I'm low as hell tonight and I didn't get the job with the *National Geographic*."

"Oh, I'm sorry."

"Get rid of Galoshes and come right down."

"I can't. We haven't even finished dinner."

"Say I'm your closest girl friend and have peritonitis."

"I will not."

"I need you, baby."

"I'm hanging up, Ham. Don't call again here."

"How do you know I won't take the pills?"

"Because I know you."

"Think so?"

"Yes."

"The hell you do. Listen, Tess, listen—why don't I come up and get you? I could come up in my wino outfit and the fright wig and I bet that'd give old Galoshes—"

"Hanging up, Ham."

The thing was he *did* have a wino outfit and he wore it to stuffy elite parties he figured were too genteel.

The fact that you couldn't explain this creature to Elton was the crux of the absurdity. She stared at her string beans and felt her face hot as though she were leaning over a stove; unreal was the only way to describe everything with Ham. What was real was Elton Bracken never asking awkward questions—Who was that on the phone?— only standing politely holding her chair for her and once or twice giving her the look of a sad bittern.

Mind if we have coffee someplace else? It's sort of stuffy in here tonight.

"Tell her how you lost your eye."

"He doesn't want to. Listen, you don't have to."

"Tell her how you lost your eye."

"He doesn't *want* to, Ham."

"Cyclops."

"Yes, Hamilton?" Cyclops always called him Hamilton; had it been feudal England, Cyclops would have pulled his forelock to Ham.

"Tell Tess how you lost your eye."

"Don't you do it. Don't kowtow to him."

"In a sex accident. Tell, Cyclops."

"The lady doesn't want to 'ear about it."

"You lousy limey. You jumped ship, didn't you? He was a waiter on the 'Queen Elizabeth'— "

" 'Queen *Mary*,' beggin' your pardon."

"*One* of the Queens; he's always around queens of some kind or another. Tell her how you lost your eye, Cyclops, or I'll go down and tell the Immigration Department about you."

He was clearly deeply in love with Ham; love shone out of his one eye. He had brought Ham Danish sardines and English du Maurier cigarettes in red tins.

"Well, anyway—"

"Just remember I've got my Permanent Alien Card," Cyclops said.

"Well, *any*way, when he was a young likely lad in jolly old England, he wasn't bad-looking, so he tells me, and he was the fancy boy of none other than the Duke of—Duke of what, Cyclops?"

"Neveryoumind."

"The Duke of Neveryoumind, who, it seems, liked peculiar sex and one of the things he liked to do was tie up Cyclops nude to a majestic oak on the manorial estate and—"

"I don't want to *hear* it, Ham."

"—smear him all over with cocoa butter and—"

"Ham, stop it. You're being just vile and—"

"And then shoot arrows at him."

"Finished? Thank you. I'm sorry, Cyclops. I apologize to you for him."

"I always wondered what exactly the cocoa butter was for."

"Cruel, cruel," she said when Cyclops had gone.

"Why?"

"He is so absolutely crazy about you."

"Oh, no, do you *think?* Oh, and the things I said. Oh, I could cut my tongue out. Oh, run and call him back, for pity's sake!"

"And you being sarcastic and funny about it I don't like either."

"Oh, I beg your royal pardon."

"Poor ugly sincere lonely—"

"Listen a sec, my dear. Who got the poor ugly sincere lonely thing *in* from Canada? Who bailed him out of the Tombs twice when the silly bugger got caught in Central Park trying to make out with a plainclothesman? Who coughed up twice for the lawyer to fix it? Who paid his rent nine months once when his unemployment ran out?"

"All right, all right, I'm sorry."

"It's not wise to judge *only* the exterior of a close friendship, Miss Adams."

"I *am* sorry, Ham."

Severely reprimanded, like in the army. And there were other areas where she dared not tread which were peculiar to his peculiar nature, like Floramae Hibble, another of his commitments (and here Tess could only find praise for him), a former Follies girl and now an elderly recluse. Every second Thursday, unless he was out of town on a job, he dined off Floramae's wretched board. And then, if it was not Floramae's birthday, then perhaps Floramae had slipped in the bathtub and wrenched her side or Floramae needed her radio fixed or would get no cheer on Thanksgiving. Such vicissitudes caused Ham to curse Floramae sometimes, yet he would immediately go to her; this was part of the dreadful enchantment of him, this genuine generous side of him, but if Tess so much as complimented him with a word about it he froze her.

Floramae was a tiny little creature with chicken-fuzz hair all bleached and fluffed out and with full stage makeup as though she might well be called to go on any moment at the New Amsterdam Roof. She wore baby blue taffeta and had a baby voice which had surface like an old record and blue varicose veins crisscrossed her little legs. Oh, she said, is it my Ham? Is it my booful?

And I've brought Tess today, Ham said.

Floramae did a little curtsy. The tiny room reeked of Floramae's lilac perfume; no window had ever let in a breath of pure air to rid it of the fumes of lilac. Around the puce walls were colored prints of dogs dressed as humans. She had bought eclairs for them that leaked what looked to be glue.

"And I'm so glad to meet *you*," Floramae said in return to Tess's overhearty greeting.

"Well, we meet at *last*," Tess crowed at her.

"Show me your knee, sweetheart," Ham said and she produced a little white-powdered knee from under frills. "Oh, it looks *better*," Ham said.

"Well, it hurts," Floramae said and put a forefinger to her dimple. "It *werts* me."

"Well, I think it's healing up, hon. It's just your old tennis knee."

Floramae gurgled. "Oh, he's my precious Ham, Ham the Second. Ham the First was my *Oscar*. Hammerstein. Not the one who wrote *Carousel;* his father."

"How was the ice show?" Ham roared. Floramae was deaf.

"Didn't go."

"Didn't *go?* What happened?"

"She didn't show up."

"I thought you told me Florence had *invited* you."

"She did. But she's a little . . ." Floramae made spiral gestures indicating that Florence, whoever she was, was crazy. Oh, the disappointment, she'd been looking forward to the ice show for weeks, her only treat in months and she had got all dressed up in her red (you know my red with the lace, oh, yes, Ham said, it's jazzy, darling) and waited and waited, and phoned and phoned, and Florence never showed up and so she was so disgusted she just went to bed with no supper.

It took a while to tell this tale and once Ham looked at Tess from behind Floramae's back and did a long pretend yawn.

"Well, she's a bitch," Ham said.

"No, she's . . ." Floramae again did the spiral nuts sign.

They had terribly sweet orange pekoe tea with the eclairs. Floramae gave a long account of the death of Susette, a beloved and trusted friend of a friend whom Ham also knew, and described every last detail of how Susette had been found lying dead on the sofa and the grief and hysteria of the friend and of the funeral arrangements. It was some time before it was made clear Susette was a poodle.

Later on (oh, it went on and on, hours, it seemed, in the stifling harem-smelling room) Ham encouraged Floramae to do her "number" for Tess from the *Cuddles of 1921;* it was called "Oh, Mr. Hobgoblin Man." It had many choruses, which all ended with Floramae wiggling her bottom, dimply hands over her eyes, and chirping about what Naught-y Mist-er Hobble-gobble-in Man was going to do to her, which in the innocent year of 1921 meant something very different than today, when the double entendre was as bawdy as some stag-dinner ballad. Tess felt her skin tighten as the poor little thing pranced around, pirouetting and reiterating this abominable phrase through the little old cupid's-bow drawn lips, while all the time Ham, behind her, was rocking with glee.

"But hasn't anybody *explained* to her it means something else now?"

"No. Why would you tell her? Anyway, she'd die of shock."

"Oh, she can't be that old and be *that* innocent."

"Darling, those old girls lived in a different age. They had their affairs and got laid but it was all very pristine and proper and no gentleman used four-letter words or told them there was *another* way of doing it."

"Oh, I think it's heartless and horrible."

"Oh, stop being such a frigging Westchester prig. It gives her a little joy, for God's sake, Tess. Stop being such an asshole."

"I don't like that word and I don't like anything about what you did to that poor little thing."

Later he said something about her being moved soon.

"Floramae? But she obviously loves that terrible little room."

Ham said she couldn't be left alone much longer, forgot she had left the hot plate on, things like that, fell in the tub; she was going to be taken to the Actors' Home.

"Does she know?"

No, he said and there came over his face that look that frightened her; the look of zest he had when a trick was about to be played on someone, like when he put on his wino makeup and came roaring into parties scaring people. He looked like a wild little boy.

No, he said but he and another friend of Floramae's were inventing a marvelous subterfuge to get Floramae into the home before she knew it.

He tittered about it. Suddenly she was furious with him; she didn't yet know why she was angry but her neck was prickling as she looked at him stretched on her couch, lofty, vain about everything, vain about his kindnesses.

"It's only your ego."

"What is?"

"You don't do these things out of affection, Ham. It pleases your ego, that's all."

"Oh?"

"You don't fool me one minute."

"I don't? Holy cow, and I was thinking I had you."

123

"It's your incrediffle vanity."

"*What* vanity?"

"In*sufferable* vanity."

"Well," he said quietly, "it's better than not giving *any*thing."

Got up off the couch, iceberg rising from the sea.

"Look, if I go around feeding old alley cats and sad old chorus girls and one-eyed queers because of vanity it's still better than giving them nothing."

"And make fun of them after?"

"If I want to."

"It's like Indian giving."

"What's it matter? If I want to hide my feelings that way or anyway I want, I will. It doesn't hurt *them*. And what do you know about me anyway? God almighty, what an impertinence you have."

"I guess I have. I'm sorry."

"What do you know about *my* feelings, about *my* inadequacies and *my* pain and *my* aloneness, and if it makes me feel cheerier to cheer up some old wreck and that's vanity, well, so what? I'd sooner do that and make fun of them a bit than be solemn and righteous and holier-than-thou and 'Oh, I'm awfully glad to meet you' and snub them."

"I didn't snub Floramae."

"Yes you did. Inwardly you did. I could feel it all the time. And you shook hands with her with your gloves on as if she had germs or something and then you're oh so *up* in *arms* about my vanity and stuff and make me the target because you're so frustrated you never had an honest-to-God real feeling about *any*one except for sex and even then it's got to be in the dark and oh, don't put the light on yet and turn your back a minute and then like Daddy taught you to always remember your manners and thank the host so 'You're sweet, Ham' and 'You're dear and gentle' and 'I love you, Ham.'"

There was only thing she could protest as untrue. "I've never said I love you, never, not once."

"Listen, if you said it, it wouldn't mean anything more to me than if you said I love your air conditioner."

"I know that. But it isn't fair to *label* me like that. Nobody has *no* feelings."

"Oh, there may be sometimes, just sometimes, a little *fee*ble—"

"God almighty, how about *your* impertinence, if it comes to that. How do you know *any*thing about how I—"

"—fee-ble, thwart-ed, moth-proof little teensy-weensy emotion you feel once in a while, poor underfed lit-tle emotion that scares the shit out of you so you squash it because oh, Christ, you might have to cope with it, con*tend* with it."

Silence. She looked at her lap. He straightened his tie in the mirror.

Then he said, "I'll tell you what's about the most you'll ever be able to contend with, *I* think. Some guy who wears mufflers and galoshes."

Then he came over, suddenly quieted down and kissed her on the neck.

"Poor starved thing," he said and went to the door. "So long, Tess."

The worst thing of all was he had compassion for her.

Whatever she felt or didn't feel, it wasn't nothing. At twelve-twenty she never required to see him again; at twelve-forty she needed him as much as breathing, and so it went on day after day as she went about the motions of getting up and going to her philosophy classes with the loss of him like a gap in her life where someone had taken scissors and clipped him out. Wherever she looked she saw the gap. She thought of ridiculous things like his lovely tan boots and his pocket nail file and the look of the child that came across his face like a film and was gone again and said volumes but all unread; she thought of being urged on to absurd lengths; she thought of being hurried willy-nilly here and there; the people he knew who came out of sideboards and linen closets where they lived and went in again and were never spoken of by him any more although at the time he treated them like kings and queens; she thought of the movies whose endings they had never seen because he was so quickly bored; she thought of losing him on escalators (he pushed suddenly ahead) and then not seeing him for days and his never mentioning it. The cessation, the release of pressure on her, was both tranquilizing and appalling. She felt as if she had been stranded in some bleak winter landscape, the one she found in a tenebrous gallery at the Frick. There she was, lost forever in this bitter gloomy scene of darkening forests and an acidy sky; lone Tess Adams.

But it wasn't true, she was only part of the things he had said in such anger; but even if only part, how could she change: how could she warm up her spirit? How can I thaw? she asked. How can I come *out?*

Suppose she went to him like a whore and let him do absolutely anything and everything with the lights on, with the shades up; would that prove anything?

No. The only possible step (it came to her in a flash, touching a zebra skin chair in Bloomingdale's, where she hid a lot) was humility. On-her-knees humility.

"I am the things you said. I came to tell you," she said after he buzzed her in, standing on the last flight up to his atelier; he had his big knotty white sweater on and said nothing but looked at her as though she had brought the laundry.

"That's all," she said. "I felt I'd rather say it in person than on the phone because you would think on the phone was one of my evasions."

She went back down, counting the steps as she went, until she got to the second-floor landing and he called down, "Where exactly the hell do you think you're going?"

And the only difference was they left the lights on and it blinded her a little less than in the dark. Later she said, "I love your air conditioner" and he had the good manners to laugh and squeeze her to him a little.

Just before he put the bedside light out, he leaned over and gave her an affectionate kiss and said, "Good night, old dear."

She got up at the very first light and as she had so many times done, dressed quickly and let herself out of his apartment. But instead of going home she went to a diner and had coffee and waited until the banks opened at nine and cashed a check and took a train to Boston.

They chose (rather Elton did) to go to the oldest museum down near Faneuil Hall, which was often practically deserted, and there, sitting on a seaman's locker off a schooner, which was clearly marked DO NOT TOUCH, she said with no further hesitation, "I've been having a very unhappy affair."

"I thought you might," Elton said.

"Did you? Did I look it?"

"Was that whoever it was that had you paged in the Washington Irving Inn?"

"Yes."

"I thought it might be."

"I'm sorry I couldn't tell you about it before."

"Why should you be sorry?"

"Oh, because you've always been honest and open with me."

"There's no need to tell me unless you want."

"You can't sit on that, miss," said a guard, coming on them.

"What you mean is she *can* sit on it but she mustn't," Elton said and when they found a bench in a drafty vestibule, he lit her cigarette for her and said, "I'm terribly glad you came up, Tess, and if it's something you want to talk about, do by all means, and if you don't, don't."

Well, it wasn't *entirely* unhappy, she told him, more that it was such a patchwork thing of ups and downs and moods and of his being crosscurrents of so many things; it wasn't that he was anything clearcut, a liar and a bastard, for instance—if he were a liar and a bastard there would be no problem obviously because it would be easy to break it off; she would not even be here now boring Elton about it —but the dangerous fact was he could be often enormously endearing and this is what, she said, frightened her. Frightened her very much last night when, after their row, he had been affectionate and dear and in fact when he had called her "old dear" the terrible thought had flashed through her that he might as well have called her "old shoe," that he was even submitting them to a semipermanent relationship and it would be frighteningly easy to go along with it and it could just go on and off and on and off for an indefinite period of time. Not that (and you mustn't get the wrong idea, Elton, and I can swear to this on a stack of Bibles) she had ever had any remote notion of settling down with him and by that she didn't mean marriage either because marriage to him would be unthinkable, misery, but it was this weakness for him—and yes, it was a huge and tremendously satisfying weakness of the flesh, but also a weakness of the spirit—which she felt drained and drained her until she was frightened, really frightened, that it would spoil her for anyone else ever and so the thought of it just drifting on/off, on/off was terrible, almost like being an alcoholic and trying desperately to stop.

I feel in danger, she said later as they stared down into the Charles River.

I am in the sort of danger, she said, that if he came around the corner now I would go off with him, truly.

Oh I don't know *what* to do, she said in the Boston common burial ground. Or rather, I know what to do but I don't know how to do it.

"Cotton Mather's buried here somewhere, I think," Elton said. He held her hand stepping over a frozen mud patch and then kept her hand in his.

"What it boils down to, Tess, is you must make a move and I don't think going away somewhere would guarantee its being over and from what you tell me he's the selfish sort of chap who will keep you in this uncertain emotional state indefinitely and as I'm sure you already know what I'd like is for us to be married, I'm sure you already know that, Tess, not that there is the slightest connection between the two but you might just think about it and I hope you *don't* think I'm taking advantage of your situation or your confidences to me, God forbid. So don't say anything now but I would like you to think about it. I don't think it can make matters any worse at this particular time in your life to consider it as a possibility. Not as a way out, dear, but just as something we both have known surely has been in the cards *anyway* for a long, long time and so . . ."

And so, because Daddy would have wanted it, they had a formal wedding in the chapel of Saint Bartholomew's and a reception afterward at the Pierre and her uncle Tom Adams, who was a bad passport photograph of Daddy, came from Seattle to give her away and two awkward Harvard boys stood up with Elton and when she said, "I, Teresa Leonie, take thee, Elton Ormond," he looked at her and nodded, agreeable to being taken, appreciative of it, and so, grateful for him beyond words, she thanked him back when they kissed and then in the blazingly overlit room they had cut the cake and just as she had been going to change and throw her bouquet a midget page appeared like the fingers at Belshazzar's feast, "Paging Mrs. Bracken," and she said seriously, "There's no Mrs. Bracken. Elton's mother died years ago," and then they had all laughed together. *Who* on the phone?

"Mrs. Break-in? Is that how you pronounce it?"

Even if there had then been phonevision she couldn't have seen him more clearly. The burnished blond hair and the trick of the sincere blue eyes; she could see the exact look of childlike zest.

"That clergyman is not ordained, by the way; he's been arrested seventeen times for performing—"

"Ham, I wrote you."

"It's lovely, darling."

"It was hard to say."

"Oh, no, it's lovely. I'm going to try it with *Ladies' Home Companion.*"

"Ham, don't. We only have a second."

"For what? What do we only have a second for?"

"Please say good-bye to me properly."

"Good-bye to you properly."

"I mean, say it once without sarcasm and nastiness."

"All right."

"Please, Ham."

"Just a second, I'm writing something down; it's a phone number in this booth here; says 'For a good screw call Letty.' "

A pause.

"Tess?"

"Yes?"

"Did you ever love me?"

"I don't know. Yes, with all my heart. I don't know."

Distinctly heard his two intakes of breath.

"Ham, are you crying?"

Click.

He had been crying. That put a beneficence on it, the gift of tears dignified everything and beautified it for her to keep forever.

On the other hand he was quite capable of pretending tears and might now be laughing. In which case she had been soundly mocked.

Which? She would never know which.

And that was exactly the way he had wanted it.

*　*　*

Panting, she had to lean against a tree. She had run nearly a mile, it seemed like. People had turned to look at her curiously, a woman of sixty-five tearing along Katonah streets; it was a wonder someone didn't catch on and try to stop her. Then a sudden summer rainstorm had drenched her; her thin chiffon dress was sopping and clinging to her, her hair twisting into wet snakes (she must look like Medusa), and she had no handkerchief to wipe her face. Her handbag, hat and everything she had left in the Katonah Country Club dining room when she had made the excuse to go to the ladies' room.

She ran on until she felt her legs turning into rubber bands. She seemed to be out of the city limits now; she was in some gloomy minipark not far from the beltway. She looked at her watch and saw that despite the bottle-green light it was only a little after three-forty.

Tucked into her belt was the soggy little piece of paper the one-eyed waiter had slipped her. She took it gently and carefully spread it open in the wet palm of her hand. Yes, it said, really said:

Ham. St Thomas. Mt Kisco 5.

Must mean five o'clock. So she had time to kill. *That* set her off laughing so much she had to hold onto the tree; the idea of having time to kill. Then, wiping her eyes with a damp hand, she saw that she was being watched by a young man who was standing by an old-fashioned green self-conduct utility truck. He stood very still, watching her with curiosity as if in this odd green light she might be an apparition even though apparitions had been banned along with afterlife.

Holding her little paper straw of hope clenched in her hand, she approached him in a smiling casual amble.

"Good afternoon," she said.

"Afternoon, ma'am," he said. He had a pleasant enough smile, not the quick baring of teeth they usually gave you.

"I wonder if by any chance you're going near Mount Kisco," she asked and said (she was so light-headed with her straw of hope that lies flowed out of her) she had accidentally got separated from her daughter on a crowded transbelt, thinking her daughter had got off with her, found she had got off at the wrong stop and now was lost.

"I see, ma'am."

Her daughter had her purse with her identification and her transport slugs and everything, so "As you see, I have been caught in the rain." She laughed.

"Where in Mount Kisco?" he asked.

"Well," she said, thinking electrically fast not to give any definite address that he could perhaps stop somewhere and check (and in the same flash she knew where she would go, she would go to Bracken; but to give Bracken's address could be risky, could be significant). "If you could drop me anywhere near the big Metromart I can easily get home from there."

"You live in Mount Kisco, ma'am?"

"Right near the Metromart," she said.

"O.K.," he said. He was quite pleasant and didn't condescend, didn't call her dear or pet or behave waggishly; helped her into the truck. It had a sticker on the door that said KINDNESS, PURITY, GRACE. "You ought not to walk around" he said as they drove off on the old self-conduct road. "They don't like you walking around here. No one walks around here."

"I know that," she said. "Oh, I was getting into such a panic and not having my papers or slugs with me, it looks so *curious.*"

"That's right," he said, "at your age."

She didn't like the way he said that.

"Such a stupid thing to do but those Transstops all look alike and I was sure my daughter was getting off behind me."

"Going to the clinic, were you?"

Didn't like that either, nor the way he kept glancing sideways at her.

"No," she said.

"I just wondered," he said. "Know Mrs. Ida Packard in Mount Kisco?"

"I don't think so."

"A very lovely old lady. She also got lost a week or so ago but they got her."

Got her. He was driving very fast now. No doubt to the nearest police precinct.

She was surer by the moment, the way he looked ahead and asked questions sideways, slyly. Like "Do you get out often?" "Live with your daughter's family?" "Who takes you around?" "Oh, it's not easy, I'm sure, to be an old person today, would you say?" When they reached the Mount Kisco turnoff there was a traffic holding pattern and he had to stop. She already had her hand cautiously on the door handle. "Oh, look," she said, pointing, "there's been an accident," and as he looked she got the door open and in the second before he turned to grab hold of her, jumped to the ground, fell onto her knees, scrambled up and ran. "Come *back,* old lady, you come back here," he called but she was already halfway up the steps to the pedestrian crossbelt.

For once she was grateful for the crowds, the streams, rivers of people she was usually oppressed by; being sucked into them, jostling and warm-bodied, was not unlike being swallowed and digested. But today she felt safer squashed into the blubbery mass of flesh standing around her on the moving sidewalk. Even so, when she stepped off it she looked around to make sure the truckdriver had not tried to follow her. It was vehemently denied, but there were rumors that handsome amounts of ration coupons were given out for the capture of older folk trying to escape their end.

She found, after some turning and twisting in the old part of the town, the little dark lane and rang the old-fashioned iron bell, which clanged deeply within the stone walls of the priory. After a time a slot in the heavy oak door opened and she was looking at the mild dimpled face of a young monk wearing horn-rimmed glasses.

"Could I see Brother Bracken?" she asked.

"Relative?"

"Yes, grandmother."

"Do you have visiting privileges?"

"Yes, I do."

"May I see your 427?"

"I don't have it with me. I—"

"Then we can't admit you. I'm sorry."

"I was here sometime last August, do you remember? I *assure* you I have a 427 card but I've mislaid my handbag and—"

"We have to abide by the law."

He was about to close the slot. There was nothing for it but to tell.

"Please. You see, I'm being 'called for' this evening."

His baby eyes blinked owlishly behind the big spectacles.

"I'm sorry but I'm only the doorkeeper."

"Surely just *once . . ."*

Well, wait, he said, and he would speak to the abbot. After a time bolts were drawn back and the monk beckoned her into the shadowy vaulted hall and the scent of everything old struck her in the face like a wave. Oh, lovely smells, long forgotten, of damp and stone and herbs, apples, onions; not like the vapid air-conditioned nonsmelling

133

air outside, vacuum-cleaned of all pollution so that there was no taste to it at all. Oh, world-gone-by smells of candles and bacon hanging and warm baked bread and vinegar and a little human sweat. Tears came to her eyes and almost brimmed over with the remembrances and nostalgia. She forgot her age; she could have been a child going into the neighborhood grocery store smelling sausages, thyme, cheese. Vanished world, she inhaled it wantonly, following the young monk down the chilly lamplit stone corridors toward the cloister. She breathed it in as she did the atmosphere of peace and tranquility and silence; perhaps a little too heavily tranquil: the serenity was visceral and a little treacly; the faces of the young monks in their cowls and habits walking silently past her on sandaled feet had the dazed look of too much prayer.

"Wait here," the monk said, showing her to a stone bench in an arch of the cloister garden where tulips and young daffodils blew about.

She caught at his sleeve. "I'd rather you didn't tell him what I had to tell you."

"We have no communication here except what is fundamental."

She saw him coming from the other side of the cloister in his brown habit, hands folded in the sleeves and his cowl back to show his tonsure. Elton. It was Elton's long neck and jutting chin and, as he approached her and broke into a smile, Elton's smile. There was nothing about him to indicate that Harry Platt had had any hand in his making.

"Hello, Granma," he said.

And what a darling little boy he had been, a golden little boy, and extremely serious and eager, winning prizes for this and that, growing up in the beginnings of the terrible times and yet remaining himself through all that uproar. But there had been a hidden spot in him. She should have recognized the signs earlier and maybe she could have averted what happened.

And then the discovery.

Harry Platt saying quietly, more in sorrow (which was worse),

Son, you are abnormal and against the times, you are not on the team.

So instead of the reconstructive process offered him, he chose to become a monk.

"Bracken," she said.

He was looking at her a little curiously and so breathlessly (but not to give anything away) she began to explain that her slightly unkempt appearance was because she had been at lunch with his Aunt Barbara and—

He held up a hand. "Don't tell me anything about the outside, will you?"

"I forgot."

"It's all right," he said and they sat for a little time in silence.

"What have you been doing?" she asked uselessly but what does one ask a monk?

Well, he was very proficient in his Latin now, read Latin perfectly, and he was in his spare time growing cucumbers.

Cucumbers! This boy who had such a dazzling IQ, who wrote such essays. She tried to look pleased.

"Are you happy, Bracken?"

He gave her a serious pained look. "Granma, we are not here to be happy. Not in that sense."

"I didn't mean it frivolously."

He smiled. "Serving is all we do."

Serving what? Who?

Enclosed in a silent bell.

He said, "I think in your day, everyone trying to be happy was part of their tragedy."

"Perhaps so."

"Everyone trying to be happy. Awful."

"Yes, maybe."

"What a pitiful thing only to have personal happiness to wish for."

"Maybe. Yes, I suppose so in a way."

"But I exempt you and Granpa from that because I think you were

135

unusual. I think of you as really *being* happy."

"Yes, I think we were."

"Did you know it at the time?"

"Perhaps part of the time."

"I think you knew it."

"I don't think anyone really knows it at the time. It's only when something's gone that you know what you had."

He looked out across the early-darkening cloister garden. "Lots of bluejays this year. Swallows, tanagers, grackles." Then, still not looking at her, "My father was a very good tennis player, wasn't he?"

"Well, he was a very *willing* one."

"I once asked my mother why she married my father and she said, 'Because he was such a good tennis player.' But then you couldn't take what she said very seriously. I don't think they were very happy."

He spoke of them in the past tense as if they were dead and she realized that they *were* dead to him.

"But you know," he said, "in many ways my father was a remarkable man. He was ahead of his time in some ways. He was one of the new race that knew that *that* kind of personal happiness we're talking about was already obsolete."

"*He* certainly wasn't a happy man."

"But that didn't matter to him. Being *right* mattered. I remember when I was about seven or eight in the Bedford house and something was going on about my Aunt Barbara and my mother came upstairs and said to me, 'Lie down now and go to sleep,' and I asked what was going on because there was all this shouting and she said, 'Nothing, nothing, go to sleep!' But I had to know and I crept out on the landing and there was a fight going on between Granpa and my father over Aunt Barbara going away somewhere and of course naturally I didn't understand the ramifications of it then but I *do* remember my father was utterly convinced he was right."

"He was always utterly convinced."

"So he could convince other people."

"Yes, he could, alas."

"I know, alas—yes, alas—but it's what they *wanted,* Granma. I think he was so effective because he knew what they wanted and he believed in it. They were all bewildered because nothing worked any more: family, marriage, religion. These are exclusive things— *my* family, *my* marriage, *my* religion—and he knew this. My father knew this and knew that there *had* to be some nationalization because they *wanted* it. The vast majority of people, younger people, wanted it and they voted it in in this huge majority. They couldn't bear the truth and horror of the world so they were relieved to accept this kind of neutrality in which there's no personal happiness, personal sex, marriage, family, and there's even a substitute religion of love which is *no* religion."

"No *hope,* Bracken."

"No *want* is a better way to put it."

"I don't believe they all wanted it, Bracken. There were thousands of people who knew and accepted that you can't go through life without some pain, some horrible things happening, that you can't be happy all the time."

"It's not enough."

"It was enough for *us.*"

"You had become the minority. No, they wanted to be . . . sandpapered down so they couldn't feel the awfulness of real things any more. So that they had no responsibilities, no guilt about anything any more, even cruelty."

"That's true," she said. "Oh, there's no horror about cruelty in the world any more."

"The thing you forget is that people like my father *absolutely* believe in the rightness of it."

A bell began tolling.

"I'll have to leave you in a minute or so," he said, "for evensong."

"Do *you* believe in the rightness of it?"

"Granma, I left it. I'm *here.*"

"Do you feel God with you?"

"Yes," he said after a minute, but looking away.

"Is God *enough?*"

He stared away, he seemed caught in the pincers of some conflicting ideas. "I have all I need. I am free here," he said.

Oh, but the only difference is you are buried in the sand inside while everyone else is buried in the sand outside. "Bracken," she said, "come *out.*"

He knew what she meant, of course. Come out and fight, give your life if need be, what the hell; you are in a glass bell singing evensong to bluejays and grackles.

"Come *out.*"

He turned and she saw the resentment at her for this forwardness, for ruffling the pool, and he said with an edge to his voice, "What could *I* do? In a world where they have no major crime, no major disease, no poverty, and everyone thinks alike and everyone loves everyone else . . . What could *I* do?"

She said, "If you could just make *one person* doubt."

He folded his arms into his habit. "No, I don't think so, Granma. I don't think I could do that."

A column of young monks carrying candles and chanting the ancient benedictions was moving toward the chapel. Their faces, lit by the flames, had the pinkly just-scrubbed look of little boys come from their bedtime baths who were going to be read a fairy story. All of them, like Bracken, were defectors.

"It wouldn't be any use my coming out now."

"Then perhaps one day."

"Perhaps."

He held up his hand in a gesture of blessing and avoidance and said quietly, "Good-bye, Granma."

Just as he reached the turn in the cloister, he looked back at her and said, "Be strong now."

So he must have guessed.

"Be glad you and Granpa had the perfect thing. You were one of the last."

The perfect thing.

She thought about it, walking across the gloomy stone vestibule;

138

she thought about how if you put the whole of a marriage onto a tape recorder there must be thousands of hours of things like did the plumbers come? anything in the paper? thought we'd have fish, that door is stuck again, must have her wisdom teeth out this vacation, anything in the mail? what time will you be home? got your keys? peas or squash or a salad?

Sometimes dear, darling,

sweet,

love . . .

*   *   *

"If it isn't—"

"Well. For heaven's sake—"

"Tess. How are you?"

And after so many years that he should come upon her when she had for the first time in memory a tiny cold sore on her lip. Otherwise pristine: hat, gloves, suit, bag, mink stole.

"This is Mrs. Fair. Mr. Hoban."

"Howdyoudo."

It didn't seem very real, here outside of Doubleday's. "Let's just get out of the doorway."

And are you in New York, Ham?

On and off. Are you?

No, we live in Bedford now.

Are you walking this way?

Well, it's good to see you.

I have two girls, she said. One's at Bennington and the other at Barnard.

You look marvelous.

So do you; not a day older.

Then Dolly Fair said she must go the other way to Henri Bendel, what a nice lunch, Tess, and give my love to Elton, good-bye, Mr.

Hoban, and they were left standing on the corner of Fifty-seventh Street. There were faint lines around his eyes now and perhaps it was only the yellow early-winter sun but his hair could just possibly be subtly blonded.

She said in a chatty formal voice, "Once in a while I've seen your name under a photo in the *Times Book Review.*"

"You must be the only one apart from the linotyper."

There was a change in him. There was a lack of bravado, a muted, subdued air about him, and when he said suddenly, "Your bag's open," lo and behold it was.

"Could we have a cup of coffee?"

"Well," she said, "I should try to get the three twenty-seven."

"Oh, there's plenty of time," he said and took her elbow. When they found a coffee shop he made a face and said, "Oh, I can't face that. I've had too much of that lately. Let's go to the Sherry Nether-land and have a drink."

"In the middle of the after*noon?*"

"Oh, come on," he said. "Are you afraid of being seen in a bar with a man?"

It occurred to her she was wearing the kind of grayish pepper-and-salt no-color tweed he had once protested he disliked her in, said she was hiding in it.

Outside the Sherry Netherland a neatly dressed man marched past them yelling, "Martial law tonight, you sons of bitches, *martial law tonight,* you goddamn bastards."

"The only city in the world," Ham said, "where the mad roam free."

Inside, when they were settled at the corner table he insisted on, she said, "Perhaps after all I'll have a whiskey sour."

Well, Tess, he said, here's looking at you.

"Cheers," she said and then like a hostess on a television show, "Tell me all about yourself, Ham."

But he seemed reluctant to talk about himself. He was fretful, looking out at the street, folding and refolding a paper napkin, asking the waiter couldn't they have some peanuts. He smoked and smoked. There was something about the beauty now that suggested the erosion of a Roman statue; there had been wind and rain and pollution in his life, she guessed, and as if he had been caught unmasked he said, "Nothing's worked out the way I'd hoped." He shook peanuts into his mouth and said, "To be candid with you, it's been hell."

"Poor Ham. I'm sorry."

Everybody said Australia was the new world so he'd gone, thinking he'd settle there, but maybe he'd got the word too late because he was disappointed to find everything Americanized and the same emphasis on "youth, youth, youth." "They aren't impressed by overseas experience; they rather resent it." Went on to New Zealand but that was chauvinistic and behind the times. "Too late for Australia, too early for New Zealand." Went back to his native Canada but he had found it both too big and too little.

"But I don't want *this* either. There's a creepy feeling here, Tess, don't you feel it? It's full of cracks and creaks and groans. It's the feeling like just before an avalanche, that cracking sound."

She thought there was a new softness about his mouth and that it was altogether like sitting with some older, more serious brother of his who was not as much fun as Ham but more restful to be with. Then he caught her glancing at her watch and put his hand over hers and said, "Don't go yet, Tess. It is so really terrific running into you," so she decided she could miss the three twenty-seven. He was into his fourth Scotch on the rocks by the time her second whiskey sour arrived and he was in the middle of a rambling tale about a rich woman who was offering him marriage and security for life and "Perhaps you should," Tess said absently and he said suddenly, "Did you ever think about me?"

"I told you I used to look for your name on picture credits."

"But *really* think about me?"

"Sometimes."

"How, in what way?"

"Fondly."

"Fondly. Jesus."

"Well, you know what I mean. . . ."

"Fondly. O.K. Half a loaf." Smiled that inordinately wry smile of his, peering out the window of the Sherry Netherland and tapping one finger on his glass and smiling brightly at people going by he had never seen in his life, would never see again, but she noticed he was blinking, he had something in his eye, blinking and wiping with the back of his hand.

"I want you to know, Tess, that"—he stopped and she waited—"you were one of the few good things."

Said as huskily as if he had swallowed a midge.

"Ham," she said and laid a hand on his arm in that useless gesture that after years tries to coax up an emotion but it was no more tender than if she had looked at her watch, which she had, again calculating her train.

"Oh, well," he said and then, "Listen, do you remember old Cyclops, my limey friend with the one eye? Well, he's got a very cushy job managing an inn down in Bucks County and it's a hell of a nice place actually, on the Delaware and with fireplaces in the bedrooms and billiard rooms with those soothing green baize tables, all extremely soothing, and I'm going down tomorrow. I'm rather in the mood to be soothed by green baize and the click of billiard balls and crackling of fires."

"You ought to stay awhile and give yourself a chance to—well—think things out and I am sure—"

"Come," he said and naturally she thought he meant they were leaving; she gathered her coat and bag and gloves and thought he was waiting for the check.

"Come down *with* me," he said.

"Oh." She was flabbergasted. She was middle-aged and had two children, she was about to say. The arguments were middle-aged.

"Look," he said, "have you ever figured out how many nights you have? I have. I've figured the damn thing out in the middle of the night when I can't sleep. If you live to be sixty you have twenty-one thousand, nine hundred and fifteen nights. Now, out of twenty-one thousand et cetera nights couldn't you spare me one last one? Look, scout's honor, separate rooms if that's what you want, if you've grown suburban and squeamish. Anything you like if you'll come, because I would so much like to be with you, have you with me for one more time in this perfectly damnable rotten life."

She had to elocute the trite speech. She was a married woman with two children and responsibilities. They were not, she had to remind him, two characters in some musical comedy; they were two middle-aged people who had gone different ways and the past was over and done with. Now, much as she hated to, she must leave this instant if she was to catch the five-seventeen, which would only just get her home in time to attend to the casserole her tired and hungry husband would be expecting.

"You misunderstand me," he said coldly, "entirely. You have not understood what I am saying."

"I could scarcely misunder—"

"Quite all right," he said, cold as marble. "I apologize for the ambivalence of my wording. Obviously I have expressed myself clumsily."

Although one cigarette was burning away in the ashtray, he was lighting another. It was terrible the way his hands were trembling; he could scarcely hold the lighter.

"Ham," she said (no compassion, told once she had no compassion, and she felt like someone who has said they cannot come to save a life, owing to a previous dinner engagement). "Ham," she said again, uselessly.

"I thought you'd understand," he said, "without making me draw graphs and without the humiliation of having to say something like 'Help.' "

So all day after the lie was told to Elton, she thought about the ambiguity of loyalty and that despite the secular laws and tradition (she put a nightdress into a suitcase, put in brush and comb) it was not humanly possible to give one's entire loyalty to one person. No, one gave one type of loyalty to one's husband, another to one's children and quite a different kind to one's friends. Well, after all,

Ham had been the very first man and there is a point in despair when one more rejection, however small, can send a person over the edge and she could not be the one to give another human being (should she take her Norell black for the evening? No, just wear the one plain suit the whole time so as not to even *hint* any provocation), to give another person whom she had once wanted, she had wanted passionately, the final push. She was filled with tenderness about it; such pity and compassion (she hoped) flowed through her, she felt as light as air. "My old friend Fanny Kingham," she told Elton, had had a horrendous run of bad luck and had to get down to Bucks County where she could rest with friends but had no one to drive her down. "Of course," Elton said. "Eunice will get my dinner. Don't give it a thought."

Of course it was ridiculous to drive back all that way. Of course stay the night.

He was the kind of man who never pressed for details and that alone should get him into heaven.

But she had flickers of conscience. Or was it just nervousness that made her imagine that Eunice in her Irish way suspected; had no gift for fish but Hibernian perception and she looked at Tess with what just might be the ghost of a smirk. Lamb chops (she told the servant to mind her *p*'s and *q*'s and her business by her tone), lima beans for Mr. Bracken, she said severely, in that she was obliged to drive a sick friend to Bucks County and if anyone called she would be back tomorrow at noon at the latest.

Then as she turned the car around in the drive, Eunice had the nerve to shoot up the kitchen window and call out, "Have a good time," and she was momentarily jittered, thought about possibly giving Eunice a blouse, how ugly people can be with their tiny blackmails; seizing the opportunity of equalizing their relationships. She ignored Eunice and drove off, posing as a friend putting herself out for a friend.

Ham was solicitous about not underlining the situation. He gave her tentative smiles and coughed his cigarette cough. Perhaps he really was grateful and perhaps God or whoever would forgive her this lapse as one supposes one forgives one's debtors.

She found the inn delightful as he had said, blue mists hanging over the river and the rooms smelling of beeswax and winter roses, and true to his word they had separate rooms but with a connecting door, which left the situation ajar. She had been immensely relieved that there had been no sordid signing of wrong names on the register because Ham was a guest, Cyclops said, giving Ham adoring love from the one eye and not having to close the blind one to what was going on.

So now, having got thus far, she felt she must go through with it to the very best of her ability and capacity. The surroundings helped, from the view of the darkening river over which a bare willow mourned to the chime and tock of the grandfather clock and the bright fire in the charming little bar where Cyclops (who was apparently manager, bookkeeper, bellboy and barman) served them cold deep nectarish martinis and there was only one other couple, who talked to each other in low disinterested tones, and she began to imagine there was a harmlessness to everything; began even to feel she might be doing something splendid. Between serving their drinks Cyclops went to a miniature piano and played undistracting esoteric tunes not identifiable enough to interrupt and yet reminiscent enough to turn the heart a fraction toward another heart. When the other couple were led into the dining room by Cyclops Ham said, "It's nice, isn't it?" "Oh, yes, I love it," she said and he looked at her in a genuine concerned way as though she were an invalid in his care and said, "You're not unhappy, are you?" "No," she said and very nearly said no, darling, no, love. The beautiful face, crinkled into cracks and lines of disappointment and failure, was so much more beautiful than the face of the young man who used to play tricks on her all the time, the one she never knew whether or not was in fits of scornful laughter underneath. Again providentially, business seeming to be as slow at Fodder's Inn as if there were an outbreak of anthrax, they were the only other couple in the large dining room, Cyclops serving with only the help of a pimply-faced busboy. There was cold artichoke soup served in silver bowls under the deep rose candles and then a little trout lying dead in parsley and endive and an exquisite veal ragout and right or wrong, Ham said, not knowing about wine, but a Nuits-Saint-Georges, and it began to be terrible how happy she felt, everything was so beautiful and sad because suppose she had waited and not rushed to Boston that day for safety with Elton, suppose they might eventually have come to this anyway, she and Ham? She might have had this older Ham if she had waited and the thought made her gloriously elatedly sorrowful and so she stopped short of the brandy that was offered "on the house" and just had another glass of wine and they sat on long after the disinterested couple had left (she was convinced poor Cyclops was the one making the washing-up noises in the kitchen; the beautiful place must be one day from bankruptcy) until Ham made the only near to personal remark up to now, raising his glass and saying, "Us, after all the years."

"Us," she said, "after all the years."

How the bitter times had mellowed and aged him, like the wine they sipped. His niceness was manifest and regular as breathing where it had once been as erratic as spring weather, coming and going in bursts and rains, sometimes nasty as hail in the face. But now just the sweet smile and being as punctilious as a bishop, standing up to pull out her chair, walking gravely behind her out of the dining room very much like lovers pretending to be married, the way he held open the door to the little coffee room where Cyclops had rushed to light the fire for them and the way he leaned toward her to catch everything she said (because of the catlike quiet of the inn, the ticking of old clocks, logs tumbling like soft words in the warm grate, the raised voice was inappropriate), leaned his chin in his hand and listened while she told him about her girls, the difference between her girls, Joan so indolent and Barbara so fierce (and suppose *they* had had a child, she thought, would it have been beautiful as they had been or would they have been punished for their luck in beauty and finding each other to have produced a tree stump?).

"Oh, Ham," she said.

146

"What?"

Nothing.

They looked at the empty billiard room with the cues stacked up and the lovely serenity of the green baize and in the little writing room (how old-fashioned, pens and ink and blotting paper) were the complete works of Sir Walter Scott.

Only once, to ask if she was cold standing on the little bridge across the canal in the night mist, only once he touched her, put an arm around her matronly tweed shoulder, and all the time she was thinking (knowing now she wanted him) that if only he had been like this when they had first known each other, she might have loved him instead of only wanting him.

There was a tremor on the skin of excitement as she laid out the nightdress on the bed and sitting in just her skirt and bra in front of the mirror she brushed her hair slowly, partly because she wanted him to have time to undress first and partly because it was a soothing sexual derivative, the brush rising and falling and her hair spinning itself out like silk, and she went on brushing but feeling her heart-beat quicken when he opened the connecting door and stood there wearing only a seersucker bathrobe and smoking a cigarette and she merely continued the even stroke of the brush, now at the back of her neck so she arched her back to get at the hair underneath and it perhaps gave her too proud a look, too much the look of a prancing horse on a carrousel, because Ham laughed and came toward her, looking at her all the time in the mirror brushing her hair, and took the brush gently out of her hand and embraced her from behind and kissed the side of her neck and put his hand on one breast and looked up into the mirror at her and said, "I knew I could get you again."

Mr. Hyde.

Never had the grin been cockier, the expression more pixie, the delight at this, the best trick he had ever played on her; the little boy was back, the wicked little boy hidden away carefully until she had been hooked, the little boy was sniggering away, chortling with mirth and crowing with conceit at how he had pulled it off. He could never deny himself the vanity of being delighted with himself when he pulled off one of his little coups; she remembered exactly the look and the giggle, hand with cigarette in front of the mouth to partly excuse his glee at himself, how fetching he was really, now wasn't he, how clever, and so then as he leaned again toward her but this time to take her mouth in his, she dodged him and picked up the brush and stooping sideways so that he very nearly went crashing into the mirror, she managed in two quick movements to reach her jacket out of the closet and get into the bathroom, where she put on the jacket and buttoned it up as calmly as she might do were this a fitting in Saks and went back into the room where he was sitting on the bed on her nightdress and she said, "Excuse me," and pulled the nightdress from underneath him and put it in her suitcase and threw in her hairbrush and clicked it shut, all this being performed with the most laconic air of boredom she could muster, and then took out her coat from the closet and he had stopped sniggering and was watching her with the look she knew would be his one of mock penitence and he asked just what was she doing, where, pray, was she going, he asked and crossed the room and stood there vast in front of the door blocking her way out and she said as to a stranger in an elevator, "Excuse me," and reached behind him and opened the door in the moment of his dumbfoundment and went out past him carrying her coat over her arm and her suitcase and heard him follow her as far as the top of the stairs, where he called out something about her sense of humor or lack of it and as she went downstairs called out very sharply Tess, come back here and stop acting like a fool.

She glanced into the little office off the reception desk and said to Cyclops, "Thank you for your hospitality. It's a charming place." She drove very fast. It was a little bit like having had lead pumped into the veins. She drove extremely fast. It felt just like cold lead had been pumped into her veins as a last remedial resort and they had said of course you won't feel it at first but we must warn you you'll feel it like hell when it finally hardens because after all, lead's lead.

And dead's dead.

And all the way up to New York and all the way from New York up to Bedford she got heavier with this leadenness, so heavy she felt she might go right through the seat and the floorboards and then as she turned into their drive saw that although it was way past two in the morning the lights were on in their bedroom and when she opened the bedroom door Elton was propped up in bed reading, couldn't sleep, he said, why'd you drive up all that way tonight? "Here's what it was," she said, sitting on the bed. "I lied to you. I met Ham a few days ago in town and he asked me to go to this inn with him for the night and there is absolutely no excuse for me whatever. I was beguiled by him as I always was, absolutely and totally beguiled. Only this time it was a new angle he had, he made me feel terribly sorry for him. I mean, he did look dreadful and he has had a rough time of it and I did feel sorry and he said among other things that I had been the one good thing in his life and he made me feel that if I turned him down it would sort of be the last straw and I suppose I must have wanted to believe him or otherwise I wouldn't have gone, would I? I suppose I've held this—what would you say?—*torch* for him all these years and so I was touched and pleased that he'd want me again. I suppose I should have known that, well, as you might've guessed he's no different at all, he's just as vain and totally sure that he can get everything he wants including me. 'I knew I could get you again' was what he said to me. That's all it was. That's all it ever was. Nothing. And so I've lied to you for nothing. I've put a blot on us for nothing. All these years I've thought to myself it was something, in spite of all the pain it was *something,* and so almost as though I owed him something, and all the time it was nothing."

She reached for the corner of the bed sheet and covered her face and was a young girl again, crying about being rejected by a lover. "Nothing! Oh, dear God, what a fool."

"Well," Elton said, "at least you've found out."

He was gazing at her over his glasses.

"Have you had anything to eat?" he asked.

"Oh, Elton"—she wept into his chest—"I love you more than life itself."

"I don't think that would be admissible"—he yawned—"in a court of law but I accept it with thanks."

Then there was that day, sometime after his sixty-fourth birthday.

Elton's voice on the tape said, "Dearest, do forgive me but I don't terribly want to go on with this any longer. . . ."

She hadn't heard the crack of resignation in him; if there had been one it was as soft as snow sliding from a hedge in the dead of night. It might have begun the day about a year before when they had been required to register for the new "retirement" plan, carrying their birth certificates and told to bring a box lunch like schoolchildren, and the stink of the old gymnasium which smelled half of carbolic and half of old sweat, and they were kept waiting in line, a long wavering complaining and frightened line of "old" people, and not given any seat, kept waiting in line for over two hours in the freezing unheated gym while from time to time young people with joyless faces handed out leaflets that read REJOICE! THE AGE OF LOVE HAS COME. So when they were finally at the table where they had to fill out the required forms Elton said to the pudding-faced youth in charge, "You have no right to treat people this way."

"That's all right, pops," the youth said.

"Don't call me pops," Elton roared, "and bring my wife a chair." He had glared at the boy so fiercely that a chair had been brought.

Then there was the day they had driven to Connecticut on an errand (but anything to get away by themselves and from their house, where they existed only as lodgers) and coming back were stopped at the state line by the young trooper.

He was burnished with polished leather, gleaming with brass. He stepped out from beside the flagpole that now always stood at the state-line checkpoints, held up a leather-gloved hand.

"See your license, sir," he asked.

Manner respectful, questions asked in the mildest tones.

Purpose of visit? Time spent? Amount of gasoline?

Manner kind. Excuse him while he checked the mileage gauge. He was one of the thoroughgoing ones. Most often they just waved you on. He marked everything down. Age, former profession, registered political party.

Then, "Do you support the government of the United States?" He was one of the eager beavers, all right, had his eye on a lieutenancy. "Do you salute the flag of the United States?" "Do you love God?" When Tess saw the tic in Elton's neck, the way he gripped the steering wheel, her heart almost fainted. "Yes, he does," she said to the trooper while Elton remained silent, his lips grimly clenched, staring ahead of him.

The trooper repeated the questions in the kindest of voices. When Elton still refused to reply, the trooper opened the door and said, "Sir, I must ask you to step out a minute."

After a moment, Elton got out of the car. The wind blew his sparse gray hair. His jutting chin pointed skyward.

"Er—sir, just stand here facing the flag and I will repeat the questions." Cars backed up half a mile now formed an audience.

The trooper repeated the questions. Elton stood at attention.

"Now, sir"—the voice was tender—"I must ask you to salute the flag."

"I will not salute the flag," Elton said.

"I see, sir. Do you support the government?"

"I will not answer that question."

"I see, sir. Do you love God?"

"I will not answer that question."

"I see, sir."

Then Elton said, "Whether or not I love God is a private thing to me and so is not to be used as a password."

The trooper was writing in his notebook.

Elton's head shook with minor palsy. He said, "I love that flag but not in the way you do."

The trooper slapped his notebook on his thick thigh. "Drive on, sir."

On the following Tuesday their car was taken away from them.

One night he cried out in the darkness of sleep and nightmare, "Oh, where am I? Where am I?"

". . . I knew it was all over when the Senator Bjelke-Petersen bloc took over and installed that smiling paper woman in the White House. But, Tess, it isn't that; it isn't even that I mind so terribly being told when I am to be taken away from you and for you to be required to behave stoically," the tape went on, and his voice was close to breaking here and there. "It's that I can't put up with *them* any longer; I've been feeling for a long while now that I can't put up with them any longer with their obtuseness and vulgarity and the loss of all logic. That's what's so terrible. I can't find their point of view. I'm in an alien world. How can we understand them when we know there's not an iota of sense in what they believe? This young girl driver I had yesterday said apropos of something or other I said that she loved everybody. How can you love *everybody?* I said it isn't *human.* But she couldn't or wouldn't understand me and after a while I got that patient pitying laugh they give you and she said that I oughtn't to think so much and that thinking's *pollution.* It just makes me—well—*tired* even to *try* to accept their philistinism so I said well, beauty is *truth* and truth is beauty and that is all ye know on earth and all ye need to know but she didn't understand that and of course she never *heard* of Keats. . . . Oh, what's it matter. They've reduced everything to a commonplace nothing. I feel dead among them. We might have been lazy and greedy and careless but we were not so commonplace and at least we had the manners to listen to another point of view—we had some grace, I think. Do you remember the day you slipped and fell on Vesuvius? And the fireworks over the Bay of Naples? Perhaps we should have been busier looking out, who knows? I'm glad it happened; thank you for slipping. I'm terribly sorry about this, cowardly of me, dearest, but I'm just too tired, Tess, I can't go on with it, darling. Well, anyway, thank you, dearest, thank you for everything, for nearly forty years. Thank you for every day, for every single bit of it."

* * *

It was fifteen minutes after five before she found Saint Thomas's church, hidden behind gritty cinder-block warehouses. Long disused, it had a ruined abbey look as she approached it under dripping trees in the greenish beginning of twilight. A piece of cardboard taped to a side door read PROFESSOR HOBAN 5 P.M. When she pushed the door open into the dark church, onto a carpet of twigs and leaves, there was a dark sweet smell of old funerals and weddings steeped into the rotting pews lit here and there with kerosene lamps and she heard in the echoing, vaulting, almost empty church Ham preaching about the spirit and scattered in the pews and toward the front of the church where Ham was speaking below the altar were about ten or twelve people, mostly women around her own age and from the same one-time Westchester, sitting in raincoats and old tweeds. A few of them turned their heads to see who had come in, furtive looks, eyes narrowed behind glasses lest it be policewomen or Ladiesaids questioning this little service (which is what it appeared to be, Ham wearing a clerical gown, arms outstretched, now talking about the spirit in and around them all), but the scene was too theatrical to be moving and too bizarre to be taken humorously and besides, she was not ready for it nor was she ready for whatever miracle drug or something Ham appeared to have taken and it could partly have been the dim yellow kerosene light but he remained incredibly young (except that even in the lamplight the hair was now palpably peroxide blond) except for a suggestion of wattles around the firm jawline and, in the carriage of him, a stooping.

Then somebody tapped her on the shoulder and it was old Cyclops. He winked at her with his good eye and beckoned her to follow him to a pew at the side, where they sat down in deep shadows. "Good girl, you got here," Cyclops said and patted her on the knee. "You're going to be all right, just you wait and see," Cyclops said in hoarse whispers. "What's it all about?" she asked.

"What's he doing?" "Oh, it's just a good deed he does here and around places to bring a little comfort; it's his nature. Always was, if you remember." "But professor of what? He can't be—" Serious, she was about to say, but Cyclops put a finger to his lips and they sat listening while one of the Westchester matrons raised a gloved hand (she may have been one of the old-time parishioners who had come here svelte and proud on Easter Sundays with her splendid children, who were now preparing to have her put to sleep) and asked if Ham could tell her was there any possibility that she might see her daughter once more and Ham hung his head and appeared to fall asleep standing up and no one moved, everyone tried not to cough or stir in order not to separate him from the spiritual influence, and then Ham spoke (sounding hoarse, as though he had addressed them for hours) and said he got the impression of Patricia —was that correct? and the matron said yes, that was the daughter's name—and that she was far away. In Washington State, not D.C., Ham said and there was a little sucking noise of joy and incredulity from the matron and those sitting with her and she said yes and yes, you will see Patricia again, Ham told her, you will be reunited but I can't tell at the moment exactly when.

Even at a distance and in the uncertain light she could tell that Ham was getting feverish enjoyment out of this parody. Perhaps he had a genuine cold but he coughed too often and, coughing, turned away, screening his face from them, with shaking shoulders that suggested to Tess it was much more likely he was carried away with mirth. Then, turning back, he gazed soulfully, Saint-Peter-like, at the pathetic little group huddled in the warped pews and gave them assurances that they would cross water to a more benign land, escape "retirement sleep," find their long-lost friend. "But do they believe this—?" Hogwash, she wanted to say, because these were people from her own background, not Hungarian peasants, but Cyclops' face was wreathed in adoration. He turned slowly to meet her look and said in a way that made her momentarily ashamed, "You see, dear, it doesn't matter if they believe it or not, it gives them a little hope for an hour or so and that's all he's trying to do. A little hope when there's no hope in this world for them, as you know. These were good people and they're very far down now."

It seemed Cyclops had a friend who worked in County Records who, in exchange for real eggs and boxes of figs and an occasional orange which Cyclops stole from the Katonah Country Club, passed computer information on these people: names of children, date of retirement, etc. "That's how we found out about you," Cyclops said and then, putting his lips to Tess's ear, said they sometimes managed little miracles, if she knew what he meant, like people disappearing. Even though it was a summer evening, the dampness and cold in the mostly roofless church made her shiver (or perhaps it was repugnance at the sight of what was going on) and Cyclops took off his raincoat and put it around her and they sat in silence until the question period ended and Ham said they would all sit a moment in silent prayer, during which time a rat approached down the aisle where once the radiant brides had come and disappeared under a fallen pew. After the silent prayer, Ham coughed again and shook for a while and then said that if they could safely convene another meeting, everyone would receive in the mail a notice of a second-hand-clothing sale. Please leave quickly and not in groups, Ham asked and seemed to be shimmering with the excitement of it all. When the last of the little congregation had gone through the two doors or crept between the holes in the wall, Ham did a little soft shoe at the altar.

"Come, dear," Cyclops said and escorted her up the main aisle as though she were being led to Ham for her first communion.

It was only as she came gradually closer to him and even in the flattering kerosene light that the shock froze her blood.

He may have had six facial jobs done on him. The result was horrifying, as though he had been taken apart and recycled, so that the eyes were now not quite on the same level and the mouth could not stop smiling and the baby flesh rejuvenated had the glaze of plastic dolls, the taking apart and putting together again with seemingly no reference to the original; it was only more or less Ham. It was the Michelangelo David reproduced by a fantastically untalented amateur.

She stood stock still.

Then Cyclops nudged her forward and as she went toward him there came this terrible sharklike grin through the tightened flesh around the mouth and the gleam of the plastic teeth; it was like one of the horror makeups he used to put on at parties. Only real. He was reaching out long arms to her; she saw the old hands unrepaired, the liver spots and white hairs.

"Tess," Ham said.

Forty-five years or more since she had met him at Lacey's party when he was this golden thing, she thought then, this unicorn prancing around her and pawing the ground and snorting at her and had taken her to bed with him and she had actually wanted to kiss his back in the morning and all he'd said was "Can you get home all right?" and really what had he been all her life? A nuisance. And he had never loved her and she had made all sorts of a fool of herself over him, still captivated by him and the enigma of him, trying to find the one sweet scintilla of seriousness in his mockery that might credit their affair with some reason. But that was never given to her, nothing; kinkiness, that was all, sportiveness, nothing else, nothing sincere.

And now (she closed her eyes when he kissed her and felt faint) Ham was gazing at her, if you could call it gazing and not squinting, with such tenderness and from the blue eyes two little droplets spat out in emotion. Unless he was now unable to control the tear ducts. "Tess, my dearest," Ham's voice said. Because it certainly was Ham's voice coming from this manikin holding her and he must have kept up with his gymnastics because the body was still firm as steel.

"Sit ye doon, lass," Ham said. "Well, now, you don't look too bad for an old girl ready to be taken away to the knackers."

Well, *that* hadn't changed. His way with the little barbs, telling her she was an old horse ready for the glue factory, but his impish-

156

ness was now creakily skittish, like an old vaudeville performer's. He rubbed his sandpapery hands together and she saw he was looking at her (it made her queasy) with sincere affection.

"You have to thank Cyclops for us finding you, you poor love; old Limey-queer here found your name on the list and when you were going from that confidential government computer clerk fag he sleeps with." Ham danced around in the lamplight, waving his arms, as though the dankness in the church might congeal him and the made-over flesh might all clot up. "Good God, Tess, I could hardly believe you could be sixty-five. I never knew you were five years older than me." Of course, the exact reverse was true. He was, she calculated, just over seventy but she sat still and said nothing, paralyzed by the beginnings of a dreadful thought, that he now, at last, cared for her. Because he was suddenly being enormously practical; they had to get cracking, he said, as he and Cyclops unfolded maps by the light of a kerosene lamp. "You are sure nobody followed you here?" he asked and was so bubbling with enthusiasm and excitement he didn't wait for a reply but went on discussing routes, this route, that route, to avoid going through Buffalo, where there was a checkpoint, asked was there a mattress for Tess in the van? Had Cyclops remembered the Thermos of hot coffee because it would be colder as they got farther north. Once he turned and said abruptly, "You know, don't you, of course you'll have immunity. They can't touch the wife of a Canadian citizen."

What was it, potpourri? Every time he came close, fumes of this scent he used clouded her with sweet stale cinnamon, a depressing scent, defeating scent, made one dreadfully sad. Why would he want to douse himself in that old sad scent?

"Dear old dear," he said, chuckling, and kissed her on the forehead. "You'll like these people."

She found voice enough to ask what people?

Why, these Canadian people he worked for, the Palmerstons, up in Lake Muskoka, about sixty miles north of Toronto. Dot and Cyril. With children grown and gone and so alone in this enormous house on this pine-treed lake which in winter froze over. "Can you still skate, Tess?" he asked and did some skating movements, cut a figure eight around the lantern. All Dot and Cyril had now, he said, was a Dalmatian and him. He helped them to run the big house and look after their several launches and sailboats and keep stock of their extensive wine cellar and their larder piled with honest-to-God food because everything in Canada was like the old days and if you were rich like Dot and Cyril there was no end to meats, cream, butter, vegetables, fruit, eggs, melons, lobster, crab, herring; homemade pies. A little saliva ran from Ham's smile. And the Palmerstons, Dot and Cyril, would welcome Tess like a daughter, well, maybe more like an old cousin. Dot and Cyril had insisted that she make her home with Ham in his little apartment over the boathouse. Cold in winter but we'll be snug enough, old dear, he said.

"Oh, there's only one thing, Tess," he said and tried to frown but no crease would appear in the stretched waxen forehead. "You don't mind, I hope, I told Dot you wouldn't mind, but you'd be expected to pull your weight. I chauffeur for them and do odd jobs around the place for my keep but you'd only be required to do sort of light housework. I told them you weren't any stuffy pampered Yank in spite of your money."

It wasn't the light housework she was thinking about; she was thinking about the incredible fact that here he was, rescuing her like an aged Peter Pan rescuing a doddering Wendy, and that he was beside himself with the excitement of it. The fact of his rescuing her and their being together forever, snug in the boathouse, and the fact that she would be living on indefinitely, on the bounty of *his* generosity; the gratitude that should be pronounced over and over to him. That was what she was thinking about. Not the light housework.

"When I told them about you and that I was going down to get you . . ." Ham was saying and then more and more about Dot and Cyril and their magnanimity in allowing Tess to come and live with them in return for just light . . .

What she was now beginning to think was quite extraordinary.

. . . and a little cooking, say on weekends when their regular cook was off, and listen, Ham was saying and rubbing her hands in his as though she were frozen, listen, it is the kind of house, the kind of life you remember, Tess, the kind of life that's finished in the U.S., the kind of beauty and dignity . . .

What she was beginning to think about was something quite tremendous.

. . . and graciousness, Ham said. Why, Dot Palmerston has a *sit-down breakfast,* Ham said triumphantly and held her as though she had been about to faint for gratitude, for her life and a guaranteed sit-down breakfast.

What she was thinking was that it was *her* life.

Whether it was to be only another hour or another ten years, whatever was left of it was hers and it was all she had and all she had ever had and Ham was appropriating it, in a way he was taking it away from her. The extraordinary thing she was thinking was that she still could, if she liked, not allow it.

". . . and you'll trip along with me every place I go to give services in Canada," Ham said.

The arbitrary way that he was dictating the rest of her life made her feel more deprived of it than by the yellow bus coming tonight to take her away to the "sleeping chamber."

She thought of waking every morning to that waxen store dummy beside her, and wouldn't there have to be some ceremony, however cursory? (and she supposed Dot and Cyril would be witnesses, Dot with a little bunch of violets to hand her afterward) and she saw herself being supported by Ham, the two old parodies they were now, in front of some justice of the peace and saying their vows and Ham gazing down at her with the smile of the savior and her giving him a look of tremulous gratitude (now kiss the bride and Dot and Cyril would titter kindly at the two old dears) and the ceremony would be a kind of blasphemy and the marriage a travesty (supposing he was going to consummate it with conceited virility in ardent lovemaking) and as a tremor of nausea went through her, she closed her eyes and thought oh, no, I'd rather die.

I'd rather *die!*

The little hyperbole so often used in her life was now true. It couldn't be the more perfect expression.

And so, with the comicality of it, she rocked with laughter, fell across her knees and backward again, laughing until the old vaulted broken arches echoed and startled birds flew up screeching. Laughed until she subsided into hiccups and gasps—uhuh, uhuh, uhuh—oh, God, she gasped, wiping her streaming face with her sleeve and then Ham said through stretched lips what's so funny?

"The situation," she gulped.

"Am I to understand . . ."

"Give me a second."

". . . you think you're too grand to accept . . ."

"Oh, not grand," she said, "not grand at all but . . ."

If he could have managed an expression, it would have been incredulity. (I *knew* I could get you again.) His eyes were dilated with disbelief. "You'd rather let them *take* you than go with me?"

What could she say? It was true. "It's not feasible."

"Why not? I'm a joke now?"

"No. Dear, no. Never. I wasn't laughing at you, I'm terribly grateful, Ham, you've never been dearer to me, but I couldn't. It wouldn't be feasible."

She put out a hand to him but he slapped it off like a spider on him and took a step away from her and she saw to her dismay that his head was shaking, that little noddings shook him.

"What am I going to tell the *Palmerstons?*" His voice cracked in falsetto. "That you preferred to go to the knackers? You preferred to have them come and take you away to the sleep chamber or whatever they call it? I see. Thank you, thank you. I see what deep respect you've held me in. Well, go and be damned, you ungrateful bitch."

He tried to stalk away with dignity and ducal pride but it was more a series of jerks. He had to hold onto the pew gates.

"Ham," she said and he muttered something about his being served right even bothering about her.

He pegged away past her in clouds of old cinnamon and stale

roses. He sat down in a faraway pew. "Get lost. Get lost," he called out to the air after a while.

"I can't, you see," she said to the air. "I can't, you see," she said to Cyclops.

"You see, he was counting on it," Cyclops whispered. "There's nobody much around any more to admire 'im and 'e's the kind what has to have that. He thought you'd be so grateful, dear. He kept saying over and over that you was goin' to be so thrilled. He was like a little boy. 'Oh, won't she be surprised, can you see 'er face when I tell 'er?' Oh, why don't you go with him, love? Don't hurt him, love. They sound like lovely people and it means so much to 'im and whatcha got to *lose?* Oh, please don't let 'im down now. He's older than he lets on. There's so little for 'im now."

"I wish I could," she said, "but you see it's *my* life too."

"He doesn't always think of that."

They looked at the figure sitting so rigid and alone, the head nodding a little, angrily, and after a while she said to Cyclops, "If you have a van, could you take me, drop me somewhere near my home?"

She followed Cyclops down the aisle. At the door she turned and hurried back. Ham didn't turn as she sat down in the pew with him.

She said, "You don't know what you did."

"Apparently not."

"No, listen. You don't know what you did, Ham. I didn't know how I was going to be able to face it. When I got up this morning I sort of made a prayer, although I don't believe in anything, as you know, but I said aloud to anything that might be paying attention that *if* something couldn't happen at the last minute to stop them coming for me then I'd like to be able to find some way of doing it with dignity. Well, you gave it to me because you gave me a choice."

He turned to her and something was lit up in his eyes as if he believed this and he believed that after all he had done something praiseworthy.

"The fact that I could refuse, Ham."

He nodded.

"Made me feel *alive.* Thank you, Ham."

"O.K."

"Thank you, darling."

"O.K."

"Thank you, darling Ham."

"Bye, bye, Tess."

Fancy being able to refuse. Fancy there being something *worse.* Fancy the upside-down way things work out. Fancy it being Ham of all people in his circuslike way who could enable her now to be walking up the lane home past the grim cinder-block co-ops surrounding her old house where once oleanders and wild honeysuckle had run riot and to feel so fortified; an intactness, wholeness and strength which had come from her refusal to run (so let them come now and take her) and she looked toward the garden in the early evening light and felt this enormous calmness, perhaps like a defector who has turned himself in. She pushed open the old rusty iron gate which had been there since her girlhood. Sane was what she felt and saw the word light up in the evening air like a firefly. What a precious word it was, what a word for this world, and she said it aloud, said it slowly, "saaaaannnnne," like music; it healed, it was like clear cold water, sane. I am sane, she said to the old rotting trees. Coming back to face it is *sane.* It is *they* who are insane and must be pitied.

Quick as light, the thought struck her that Harry Platt should be pitied. But to find a way would be asking God for two miracles on the same day. She strolled up her driveway, relishing the feeling of squandering the little bit of time left; there was a pale sweetness of arbutus still left somewhere and she was breathing it in when Barbara squealed from the door oh, Mother, oh, *Mother,* is it you? Oh, she's here, she's here, Barbara called back into the house and ran down the pathway saying urgently Harry's been terribly angry, I want to warn you he's furious, Mother, we thought you'd run off somewhere, Mother, you shouldn't have done it. Oh, goodness, Barbara said, touching her, you are damp, did you get caught in the rain? "You better change your dress before you catch cold," said insane Barbara, poor psycholobotomized Barbara, who could no longer see paradoxes, could no longer see any foolishness in urging her to change her clothes so that she would not catch cold en route to the death chamber.

"Never mind," she said. Poor Barby. Thinking, I don't have to say good-bye to her. I said good-bye to her, to the real one, years ago the night they took her off to Sea Island.

She went into the house with Barbara shambling behind her saying Harry would be relieved, Harry had delayed going back to Washington, Harry had been in touch with the police.

"All this fuss over me?" Tess said.

The fact of their concern was obvious. It might have leaked out in high circles that the great Harry Platt's mother-in-law had actually got away.

But I must remember that I am sane, she thought, *I* am the sane one.

"She's here, she came back," Barbara called to Harry, who had opened the study door and was standing there with two military policemen, and Barbara tried to steer Tess toward them but Tess went calmly on past the policemen staring at her, this senile wandering creature in these wet clothes who had been roaming around by herself against all the rules. She ignored their quick-fire little bursts of questions popping around her like ack-ack. "Mother, come here," Harry barked but she went calmly on upstairs and feeling once more mistress of the house even though, opening her bedroom door, she found that everything was gone, stripped; furniture, draperies, everything had been taken away in a great hurry, possibly in preparation for any official inquiries into her running away. Harry had begun a provisional nonexistence for her. There was no end to their statistical self-deception.

"Tessa," Harry's voice called. "Come down. I want to speak to you."

The voice of authority, the voice of America.

It was like deep breathing, this feeling of peace and calm that enveloped her now that she had accepted her end. She was completely in control of herself. She opened the window and looked out as if it might have been twenty years ago and Elton down there doing a little weeding and she was once more mistress of this house and these others were children, unmannerly children, disturbed children who had taken over her house, her world. But children just the same. She left the empty bedroom and crossed the hall to the master bedroom, where Joan was sitting, still in a sedated condition, in a high-backed wicker chair looking out the window, her gaze as vacant as its glass. There was probably no use in saying it but she felt the reflex of motherhood kick in her.

She said, "Listen, darling, can you hear me, can you understand me? I have to go in a few minutes and I want to say something to you. Joan, leave him. You must leave him. Find a way. Agree to anything he wants but *leave* him. Even if you have to go to one of the divorce colonies you'd be better off. Leave him, darling. Can you hear me? Can you understand me?"

Joan nodded. She may or may not have taken it in. Joan nodded slowly so she might just have taken it in. On the other hand she may have been thinking about doughnuts.

Tess kissed her lightly on the forehead and went out, closing the door, and went downstairs to face it.

The police officers were gone and Harry was smiling his charming smile. So, he indicated smilingly, she was forgiven this lapse; he was insufferably kind. "Have a nice walk?" he asked. He stood there in his old-fashioned conservative sixties suit, looking shorter than ever because he was reduced in importance to her, he was small fry, trivial, pathetic.

She walked right past him, ignoring him, into her own drawing room as though it were twenty-five years ago and he was that eager aggressive little interloper gate-crasher.

She saw by the little gold clock on the mantel that it was a quarter to seven. So she had fifteen minutes or so before the bus came for her. She saw her handbag was there, having probably been searched, and she took out lipstick and comb. There was no reason to go looking a fright. All the time Harry was saying in the background that of course they had been worried out of their minds about her going off by herself like that at her age and so he had had to invent stories to cover up for her. There were rules nowadays; the ship couldn't be run without rules.

She let him run on (he was even tender to her, tapped her gently on the knee, asked her would she care for a drink, Scotch and soda) and listened politely like a fatigued hostess with a guest who is staying too long and then quite suddenly without warning she sent the shot directly across his bow, as it were.

"I saw Bracken today," she said. "I saw your son."

Harry's head jerked backward from the invisible uppercut to the jaw and he put a finger quickly between his neck and his collar to prevent choking. He crossed the room toward her in his stiff pegleg walk, arms swinging.

"Now, Tessa, Tessa, I got in specially for you a beautiful bonded bourbon if you'd rather—"

"I went to the monastery and saw Bracken, your son."

Then the beck, the nod, the smile of the church usher.

"But I don't have a son."

"He might be the only thing you could've been proud of, Harry."

"Alas, I have no son," Harry said, smiling, smiling.

"If you could understand character and conviction and things like that, you might be proud of him."

"No, I never had a son."

"He's kept his convictions."

"Joan and I had no children."

"Anyway, he defied you."

"No children."

"Defied you all."

"None."

"One day maybe he'll come out and defy you to your face."

"In my high position having children wasn't advisable."

"In the long run, he may come out. Everything happens at last."

"Being in high public office, I set an example by having no children."

"Bracken said you were a remarkable man in some ways, that you could believe in anything and you could make other people believe."

He was smiling still but he could not stop one eyebrow from twitching up and down and he was turning away and glancing out the window as if he was hoping to catch a glimpse of the bus coming in the gate, as though the bus might save him. When he turned back to her she saw what she'd told him Bracken had said had touched him in some remote district of the soul kept with the strictest maximum security.

"I hope I have persuaded people for their own good," he said.

"I believe you believe that, Harry."

"I believe I have made a contribution to society," he said and gave the oatmealy smile she so detested. "I think I may say I've done enough to make a little scratch in history."

And somebody had come up, laughing fit to kill, and said to her and to Elton oh, come and look at this odd boy, crazy boy, playing tennis like Jacques Tati. Everyone was laughing at him but he was intensely serious. The way he whacked the balls with this ardor and this terrible dedication, he was going to get somewhere.

And he didn't see that he was a pitiable thing and he couldn't see it now because he had long ago blended into the society he had helped to create. He was one of those people who had to win the game even if it meant making up the rules. Someone had once said that these people were sometimes forced to feel they had missed something (it had been, now she remembered, Zina Edwards who said perhaps it wasn't fair they should be forced to feel they had missed something, like love, for instance) and was it the mention of Bracken and Bracken's cold admiration that had set off this alarm bell deep in Harry which was ringing its head off in the dead of night in Harry to announce a fire of doubt?

Was it fair game to force Harry to feel he had missed something?

Was it cruel to say, as she heard herself saying sincerely, like a mother, "What potential you had. What a pity you didn't make something of it"?

The alarm bell must be deafening, the way he raised his voice to hear himself.

"Well, you don't think being on the White House staff is important? You don't think writing the President's speeches is anything much?"

"You write a lot of hogwash for somebody who doesn't exist"— he held up his hand to stop her; the eyebrow was flicking madly— "and it's all a lot of fine-sounding Jabberwocky and you know it. You are too bright not to know it, more's the pity."

He waved her quiet. "Quiet now," he said. "Don't do that, Tessa. The last resort for losers is to demean."

And they had demeaned him over and over again; the times they had snubbed and deliberately insulted him and he had gone on quietly unheeding, eating his way into their house as softly as a termite. And she was thinking of the Sunday afternoon when she tried to get rid of him for good. The Sunday he came ringing doorbells all over the house until she was nearly crazy, rang and rang to be admitted, to be accepted, and she had been frightened by his terrible determination to be one of them and she had flung open the door and screamed why do you bother us, what do you want? We don't want you here, go away, go away.

And he had given her that look of a whipped dog being driven away into the blizzard. Crawled away like a poor whipped dog and found the other whipped dogs. All the whipped, abandoned, homeless dogs joined themselves into a pack and ran loose in the land and took what they wanted and said among themselves now we know how to be a group; we will go back and ravage the homes where they wouldn't give us crust nor bone.

"I wonder," she said. "If I hadn't driven you away that Sunday you came ringing at every door in the house, if I had been just a little kinder, maybe everything would have been different. You wouldn't have wanted to get back at us, at everybody, Harry. You might have taken a different course. You might have *really* made something of yourself."

He had become very red and was holding his chubby little hands pressed tightly into his crotch.

"Nothing would've been any different. Nothing."

"If somebody had been kinder—"

"Nothing." He almost shouted it to be heard above the fire alarm in him. "I belong to my time and don't you forget it. I belong to my time. Otherwise I wouldn't be here and if I am something demeanable to you, some kind of rascal, look what rascals you were to me and my generation with your money and your snobbery and your selfishness toward your fellow men."

Now he spilled out his snippets of Jabberwockery, snips from the speeches he wrote. It was his style exactly.

"So you sat in your churches with your hypocrisy and miserable ethics polluting the land and the spirit and gave people nothing. It was time for somebody like me, like *us,* with the true spirit to come along and give them something and you *know* what we gave them. Practical religion, ration tickets and hope, and now there is not a polluted lake in the country, not an unclean stream. There is no cancer and no heart disease, a *min*imum of crime, *no* poverty and *national* mental health, and we have accomplished all this in little more than ten years. We have been viciously attacked and maligned by certain minorities who stir up trouble but we have never flinched from our sacred trust and duty, remember that. Be*cause* it was time to do it. We have changed everything because the time had come to do that—it was time."

His time, he meant. He'd come along at the exact right time. It was possible certain people did. Were created by the times themselves for some purpose and she was thinking that perhaps there was a strategy to societies forming and unforming themselves and that perhaps the dark winds that blow across this terrible world are not without reason. But winds can change and she had a sudden vision of Harry in the future. It was as if she were seeing him, looking very small and sitting alone in some immense room and still talking this way about himself and his time and no one there to hear, ousted or ostracized perhaps because of a change in the wind, alone and extolling himself, telling the empty air he had never wanted this or that in life, he was complete.

Now he seemed to be waiting on tiptoe for her to say something, his eyes boring into her. "Well, anyway," he said, "nothing *you* did or said would have made any difference. It was history." So, there. So, he had sat down with kings and presidents. "Well, anyway," he said (had to say because she didn't), "I've come a long way from the days when I used to bring the ice cubes, wouldn't you say?" He flashed her his smile, that automated smile that was both scintillating and triumphant, and whatever tremendous effort he had used to put out the fire of doubt welled upward in him to escape into one tear which hung on an eyelash like a star. It hung there, she felt sure, for reasons that only Harry Platt once knew but had probably forgotten long ago, deliberately doused; some other part of Harry Platt that might possibly have been human and decent but was not requisite to the necessity for triumph, not related to the desperate need for honor and glory and so stifled, and she saw (the tear hung there, he seemed unaware of it) he was subconsciously aware of some failure, that he was still that desperate boy hurling himself around a tennis court, still begging her for a crumb of respect, having to remind her he once brought the ice. He was really no further ahead in his ambition for himself in spite of all his triumph in the society he'd helped to create. He had never been important, only successful; never honest, only candid; never cruel, only petty; never intelligent, only shrewd. And he had never enjoyed himself for an hour in his whole life.

She saw this as brightly as the blazing headlights of the yellow bus searchlighting the room as it pulled into the drive.

"Poor Harry," she said and meant it, astonished at the engulfing feeling of compassion for him, wanting now after all these terrible years to say she understood what his needs had been and how they had gradually stunted and throttled him like vines. With the ecstasy that comes with forgiveness, warm tears ran down her face, she who

169

had been told she could only cry cold tears for herself, and now she cried for Harry. She had been granted this peculiar miracle at the last moment to cry salt tears of compassion for poor, stunted, barren Harry Platt.

"Poor Harry," she said and touched him lightly, but he drew back and saw her sincerity and flushed with dismay at it and so they stood two worlds apart until an aide came in and coughed politely and said that they were waiting for Mrs. Bracken, the bus had come to take Mrs. Bracken away.

She went out of the room and crossed the hall in a kind of exaltation at the knowledge of her own life.

Outside, the old yellow bus was waiting (someone with a clipboard was reading out her name and draft number; old faces both resigned and terrified were pressed to the bus windows) and she felt nothing about this because what was going to happen now was, after all, nothing. But what had been was infinite. She knew with a kind of wild joy as the moment capsulized her whole existence in a bubble just the size of Harry's tear: What had happened to her was what was important. Birth and pain and joy and grief and terror and boredom and expectation and Elton saying thank you for slipping on Vesuvius and Daddy saying darling, nobody's happy but try to have a good time. That was what mattered and she was filled with the elation of it, like a song, and all around her the earth and sky were filled with it, it was the song of life. Oh, wonderful and terrible. How terrible not to have lived it. Not to have experienced all of it.

Not to have lived through every moment of it, everything.

Even this.

Even this, now.

Now.

She was lifted up with it. She ran toward the bus.

75 76 77 10 9 8 7 6 5 4 3 2 1